D1086569

About the Author

David Ellis has worked as a doctor in the UK's National Health Service for more than twenty-five years. He was an undergraduate at St Peter's College, Oxford and then a research scholar at Worcester College. He moonlighted from the Department of Experimental Psychology to work with Steven Berkoff's London Theatre Group. His first exposure to publishing was when writing on music technology to supplement his medical school grant. He has written books on medical computing and using computers to make music, and also co-authored a book and software package to teach anatomy to medical students. He lives in North London with his husband and two cats, Basil and Sybil. This is his third novel.

David Ellis

WET & WILD

AUSTIN MACAULEY
PUBLISHERS LTD.

Copyright © David Ellis

The right of David Ellis to be identified as author of this work has been asserted by him in accordance with section 77 and 78 of the Copyright, Designs and Patents Act 1988.

All rights reserved. No part of this publication may be reproduced, stored in a retrieval system, or transmitted in any form or by any means, electronic, mechanical, photocopying, recording, or otherwise, without the prior permission of the publishers.

Any person who commits any unauthorized act in relation to this publication may be liable to criminal prosecution and civil claims for damages.

A CIP catalogue record for this title is available from the British Library.

ISBN 978 1 78455 009 7

www.austinmacauley.com

First Published (2014)
Austin Macauley Publishers Ltd.
25 Canada Square
Canary Wharf
London
E14 5LB

Printed and bound in Great Britain

Acknowledgments

As observant Islington residents might recall, there actually was a pet shop called Wet & Wild on the Holloway Road, but it closed down years ago and the premises became a takeaway.

Chris Maguire MRCVS gave invaluable advice on veterinary matters.

Monster Fish Keepers and Reptile Forum UK were helpful sources of information on caring for electric eels and chameleons, respectively.

The London Zoo press office efficiently dealt with my enquiry about how they might deal with an escapee electric eel.

The London Fire Brigade gave me the run down on the equipment they routinely use and how they would use a multidisciplinary approach for tackling unusual domestic situations where rescuing people and pets is the priority.

International Airlines Group were clear they couldn't allow a chameleon on board one of their planes, even if in first class and featuring in the act of an internationally renowned artist.

Islington Council confirmed they would be able to accommodate the remains of a chameleon in their pet cemetery, but they weren't sure about managing the outpouring of grief.

The idea of using a virtual mannequin for the therapist in Chapter 5 came from multiple exposures to the infection control nurse on duty 24/7 in the atrium of University College Hospital London.

My husband, Henry Andrews, patiently and intelligently read the first draft and I'm indebted for his comments; he'd make an excellent proofreader.

Introduction

Britain is a nation of animal lovers – or so we are told. According to the most recent survey (2013), British households host six million dogs and eight million cats. Goldfish are even more popular, with eighteen million swimming around in a goldfish bowl somewhere in Britain. Exotic pets have also become highly desirable and as many as a thousand such species are kept privately in Britain, including venomous snakes and big cats.

Buying pets has also become remarkably easy. On one particular website, at any given time, there are fifty thousand pets for sale.

But having a pet carries a responsibility and often that responsibility proves too much. Sometimes this means pets are simply cast aside like rubbish. In 2012, a hundred thousand dogs and a hundred and thirty thousand cats in Britain needed rehoming – or euthanising.

This book takes as its starting point a fairly traditional pet shop – the sort where one would go with one's children to buy a puppy or a kitten – but then adds a "what if?" to the equation.

What if a pet could take revenge for the way it was cared for?

What if a pet wasn't quite what it said on the tin?

What if there was more to the pet shop owner and his assistant than met the eye?

So welcome to my pet emporium, 'Wet & Wild', where nothing is quite what it seems.

Chapter One

Brian

The Elliott family are mostly sitting down to a meal in the kitchen of their council house in North London. As usual, Mr Elliott is disgruntled by the behaviour of Brian, aged ten, the youngest of the four children.

"Brian, you little shit, come and sit down at the table!" ordered his father.

Brian was sitting in the corner staring at the cat. He didn't respond.

"Brian, listen to what your father is saying!" instructed his mother.

He still didn't respond.

"He's playing with that frigging cat again!" exclaimed his father.

Brian was *interacting* with the cat but he didn't regard it as *playing*; in fact, this was a full-on pow-wow to plan a strategy for world domination. A cat's gaze was inscrutable for good reason, as time and patience is required for the transfer of data to complete. The conversion of ideas and thoughts between species couldn't be rushed or else it became a meaningless jumble.

Brian returned reluctantly to the table and tentatively applied a knife and fork to the lump of meat that passed for supper in their household. Unfortunately, he'd known its owner and even barely touching something so dead and overcooked felt like stabbing his best friend in the back. Not that he had a best friend – of the human kind, anyway.

"Dad, Brian's not eating his food. Can I have it?"

The inquiry was coming from the first in line to the family misfortune. She was an overweight girl of fifteen who went by the name of Julie and was generally reckoned by her peers to be easy with her virtues. And she was a pig. Brian had once tried communicating with her in the way he would with the real thing. He actually detected a glimmer of response and noticed that her food intake had increased massively ever since.

He'd always suspected there was something strange about his father and this had confirmed it. His taunts of "oink, oink" when he was in his dad's earshot had no effect, however.

"That's not fair!" Jason shouted, second in line and a skinny, accident-prone boy (well, that's how it was always put to the police) of fourteen-and-a-half who was good at getting into locked buildings but not so good at getting out of them.

"Julie's always getting Brian's leftovers!" he added angrily.

Which was true, but she was only getting what befitted her low-life standing in the world.

Then there was Sherpa, aged eleven, and named after Sherpa Tenzing Norgay during a brief phase of fantasy when his father considered abandoning life on the buses and becoming a world-famous explorer. He decided to end further discussion by simply grabbing the meat from Brian's plate with his fingers and stuffing it in his mouth. He was the biggest pig of them all.

That snapshot was typical of mealtimes in the Elliott family; he or she who shouted loudest or grabbed the hardest got the most food. So, Brian retreated to his corner, scrunched his eyes closed and put his hands over his ears. If he concentrated he could hear the sound of blood pumping through his arteries and that made him feel a little more alive again.

****

It's difficult to say exactly when Brian first discovered his talent with animals, but he started experiencing non-human communication just after he commenced toddling. The elderly cat in question didn't have the patience to interpret his babyish noises and returned to her grooming routine after a disdainful sniff of his nappy.

A pivotal moment was at the age of six, when a goldfish arrived in the family home in a plastic bag. It wasn't a happy fish. His father had dropped it on the table after finding it left behind on a seat on his number ninety-one bus, presumably after being won at some fair. It probably wouldn't have survived another round trip on the bus, particularly if someone had sat on it. Figuring even the most meagre source of protein would end up being eaten by something or someone in the household, Brian intervened.

Brian picked up the bag and gazed at its occupant and for the first time in millennia, a goldfish held a human's look. But it didn't just gape in the disinterested, what-the-hell-are-you-looking-at-me-for way goldfish are renowned for the world over; it actually *stared* for a good five minutes until Brian broke the connection.

A goldfish's pouting mouth speaks volumes – if you understand the non-verbal language. Goldfish are particularly interesting because there are many of them and most of the time they swim around doing little but thinking a lot. That's in stark contrast to dogs that do a lot but think very little, apart from the best ways of sniffing crotches and expressing separation anxiety.

What most people don't realise is that the underwater world is actually a worldwide web. The big fish like whales are the Google-type servers and smaller fish act as mobile nodes sharing the information wherever it's needed. Dolphins are particularly helpful because they're quick on the uptake and naturally friendly, although they almost spilt the beans to humans about the underwater network. That's where the so-called 'song' of the humpback whale came in handy; a highly compressed, infrasonic data stream designed to stop prying cetacean scientists from discovering what whales have been up to all these years. It's efficient and means a fish brain like that of a goldfish, with a mere five million brain cells, can tap into an unlimited information source and appear very bright. In fact, goldfish would make good doctors because they're also patient and won't look at their watches when the consultation reaches the ten-minute mark.

During the brief time Brian was in communication with the goldfish, he got a good impression what it was like to be living through two millennia of boredom away from the family shoal of the Jin Dynasty. The goldfish couldn't put it into words, but it was a feeling of loss and abandonment and generally being pissed off, which is just how Brian's father behaved most of the time. Unfortunately, his father didn't belong to any exotic dynasty apart from a long line of pissed-off, Transport for London bus drivers.

Brian used some of his pocket money to buy food for the fish and he found an old plastic container discarded by his mother to keep it in. Once the goldfish was looking healthy, he persuaded his mother to take him to a park where he knew they kept carp. While his mother's back was turned he surreptitiously emptied the contents of the original plastic bag into the pond. The goldfish didn't exactly blow him a kiss, but it hovered for brief moment at the surface of the water, pouted sincere thanks and goodbye, and Brian knew he'd done something really good. What Brian couldn't have known is that Ebenezer III (the goldfish's ancestral name) was already on his way back to the Jin Dynasty *ca.* AD 400, courtesy of a wormhole that had conveniently opened up at the bottom of the pond. Like the phenomenon of crop circles, spontaneously vanishing ponds remain one of life's little mysteries.

****

Following the trans-universal exodus of his goldfish, Brian dedicated the next few years to seeing what he could achieve with other animal species. Invertebrates were the worst of the lot and slugs the absolute pits. Buzzing insects seemed pre-programmed to annoy and to do unpleasant things to cat food. But he was fascinated by insects belonging to a hive or colony like honey bees and ants. Individually, a bee's brain didn't amount to much, but once in a collective they could almost take on the Borg if they wanted to protect their queen. Brian realised quickly here was a critical mass of the right brain cells needed for him to make headway at communication.

Birds were a challenge – chickens in particular – but large birds like parrots were much more interesting. His aunt had a very fine specimen of an African Grey, but it suffered from an excess of EastEnders, so communication with the bird was like being stuck with a busty woman pulling a pint.

****

Brian's most significant claim to fame happened when he was twelve. He was walking home from school in the gathering dusk through a park and noticed a bag lady with her overflowing supermarket trolley. Half-a-dozen dogs that obviously weren't out for walkies or to do their number ones surrounded her. The woman started picking objects out of the trolley randomly and throwing them at the rabid mob, which just incensed them further. They probably detected Diamond White cider on her breath as well. One dog barking at full volume is bad enough, but six create an experience which is both ear splitting and terrifying, even when you're sozzled. Brian could see the fear only too well in her bloodshot eyes. He could also sense the thrill of the chase in the leader of the pack, an Irish wolfhound clearly brought up to know better judging by its immaculate grooming. However, put perfectly nice dogs together with the right stimulus and you get a fearsome attack machine that will stop at nothing.

Brian realised at that point he had to do *something*, whatever the consequences might be. He approached the dogs in what he hoped was a confident manner (in other words, copying his dad's macho stance when dealing with troublemakers on his bus) even though he felt nothing of the sort. Now the thing about dogs is that they follow their own moral code, which is all about doing whatever's necessary to maintain the pecking order and receiving a pat on the back for doing it. Throw a dog a ball, give it a treat, do that a few more times, and you've helped establish you are the alpha male. Reinforcement is the name of the game. At that moment the dogs were breaking the moral code simply because the top dog had engaged a primitive instinct for some non-specific reason.

To stop it, Brian needed to break the chain of command, which is tricky when your hormones are going haywire and you've got a squeaky voice.

"HhvvmmcccckkkkTTSSSS" was the strange, strangled sound that emerged from Brian's mouth. This was initially from his throat but built to a crescendo of consonants extending up into the higher frequencies only dogs can hear. Overall, it was a bit like using a dog whistle for catching a dog's attention, but much more focused. To start with, the long "Hhvvmmcccckkkk" broke the chain of command and was the equivalent of a STOP sign in the Highway Code. The "TTSSSS" at the end essentially instructed the dog to FRIG OFF. Which is precisely what the pack of surprised dogs did when Brian opened his mouth. In fact they ran like there was no tomorrow, leaving the bag lady astonished she'd escaped unscathed and also wondering where the next bottle of Diamond White was going to come from. She scrabbled around on the ground looking for any coins scattered unintentionally in her panic.

"Are you okay, lady?" Brian asked helpfully.

"Yeah, 'cause I am, no thanks t'you, you fuckin' prick. Mean you jus' standin' there makin' weird noises when them dogs could've 'ad me fuckin' legs off."

Great, thought Brian. You employ the most advanced communication technique known to animal kind and that's the thanks you get from someone who can't even pronounce her words properly. He'd heard that sort of thing expressed before but never with so much venom behind the delivery; perhaps he should have let the dogs get on with the job.

But Brian did have an admirer, a jogger who'd videoed the entire incident on his mobile phone and was already in the process of uploading it to Facebook, his Twitter account and a friend at the ITV, with the tagline 'Dr Doolittle?'

It didn't take long for questions to crop up about the identity of the boy who'd so bravely saved the ungrateful bag lady. One of the people who responded was Brian's father who was quick to seize any opportunity to make a fast buck, even if it involved a member of his own family whom he customarily regarded as a waste of space. In fact, he'd been aware for some time there was something weird afoot between Brian and animals, so he wasn't that taken aback to hear about the incident in the park.

****

It took some persuasion to get Brian to agree to appear on *Good Morning, London!* but appear he did with his mother holding his hand as instructed by the programme's director. It wasn't an auspicious start to Brian's fledgling media career, even if he was wearing his best clothes and had his hair combed by the makeup lady. Carefully worded questions about what he did and how he did it were met with a "yeah", two "no's" and a grunt, which could have meant anything. Then one of the interviewers had the bright idea of asking him to demonstrate on camera what he'd actually said that had caused the dogs to run off. Brian looked at his mother briefly for approval and she nodded. The "HhvvmmccckkkkTTSSSS" that emerged from the innocent looking child's mouth was one of the weirdest sounds to have made it across London's airwaves for a very long while.

Dogs usually couldn't give a toss about what's shown on breakfast TV, but on this occasion many thousands of dogs across inner and outer London simply dropped what they were doing – gobbling down food, licking their genitals, chasing the cat, etc. – and sat bolt upright all ready for the next set of instructions. Unfortunately, one of the limitations with low definition TV is the audio bandwidth, which means anything above ten thousand hertz doesn't make it past the TV speaker. So what started out in the studio as a series of commands to STOP and then FRIG OFF ended up as just the STOP alone, which left all those dogs stuck in their tracks. Over the next hour or so, normal function was more or less resumed, but it left some dogs deeply traumatised and wondering where the hell the top dog had gone to.

The consequences of the brief but dramatic TV appearance were many and varied. Someone from the BBC offered Brian a screen test for a children's TV programme, but it was clear he'd fail at the first hurdle of being able to read coherently from the autocue. A psychologist, who should have known better, popped-up on TV with his sound bite analysis and volunteered the diagnosis of Asperger syndrome. That had delighted his father who'd long since wanted a more definitive label for his son than simply 'odd' and thought that bad genes on his wife's side explained everything that was amiss with their children.

So, before Brian could utter, "HhvvmmccckkkkTTSSSS," he found himself back in his best clothes and on the way to see a child psychiatrist. An animal lover herself, Dr Virginia Dodgson was keen to discover more about Brian's unusual connection with the animal kingdom.

"Brian, when you were on TV you made a funny noise. Can you do that for me now?"

Brian looked at his mother and she nodded.

"HhvvmmccckkkkTTSSSS."

Dr Dodgson looked taken aback, as were all the dogs in neighbouring houses who shot out of their dog flaps. Her own Pomeranian in his basket next door misinterpreted the command and tootled off with an erection in search of the nearest bitch on heat.

"That's... er... very interesting, Brian. Where did you learn that from?"

Brian looked down at the floor.

"Go on, Brian, tell the doctor!" ordered his mum.

"Dunno," he mumbled eventually.

"Yes, you do! Tell her!"

"A cat told me," he muttered under his breath.

"Did you say a cat told you?" asked the disbelieving Dr Dodgson.

"Yeah..." He looked down at his feet. He noticed he hadn't done up his laces properly, which was always a bad sign. "And Ebenezer the third added the details."

"Who is Ebenezer the third?" the doctor asked with mounting irritation. She was also wondering why it had gone so quiet next door; her Pomeranian had a habit of barking on every quarter hour.

"A goldfish."

"A goldfish?" queried Dr Dodgson with an emphasis that would have done Lady Bracknell proud.

The psychiatrist decided to get Brian to talk about his other interests, in the hope that it would loosen his tongue. In order of merit these included: haiku poetry, Japanese greeting rituals and the constellation of Leo (allegedly the ancestral home of *Felis catus*). There were more but these were the ones uppermost in his mind at the time. He'd set himself the exacting goal of writing a different haiku poem for every animal species he met. By the time Brian felt he'd given an adequate account of these interests, Dr Dodgson was snoring and his mother had gone out for her umpteenth fag break.

The long and the short of the assessment was that: a) Brian could possibly be mad (well, suffering from early-onset schizophrenia with some obsessional features); and b) he probably was Gillick competent (a long story, but relating to an overbearing mother who didn't want her under-sixteen child to go on the oral contraceptive pill; so if a kid like Brian says no to treatment then no it is).

Brian's view was different, he simply preferred communicating with animals than people and admired the economy of means the animal kingdom generally used.

****

Brian was a voracious consumer of the written word as it made more sense than listening to someone's inefficiently delivered drivel. That view included his long-suffering teachers, most of whom had given up trying to engage him in class. Curiously, his module marks weren't bad and certainly sufficient to get him a handful of GCSEs. When Brian wasn't in class he'd be reading or searching on the internet. His interests ranged far and wide but tended towards subjects which were esoteric or where some element of control was occurring. One of these preoccupations was the sixties invention of the 'disk jockey': initially someone who simply jockeyed singles into place on radio station playlists, but latterly elevated to superstar status and commanding massive fees. Brian thought the most interesting of these was Piotr Thom, a Polish immigrant of humble beginnings, but with an impressive ability to communicate through music without having to say very much to his audience. That resonated so much with Brian that he'd soon absorbed every detail he could glean from the internet about the DJ's career.

From time to time Brian tried emulating Piotr Thom's ability to command an audience, but with animals rather than humans. Dogs were easy fodder but cats needed to be persuaded to stir from their basket or their favourite place on the windowsill. Brian found a combination of four inducements usually worked: a) the promise of world domination; b) an opened tin of tuna; c) a roll in some catnip; and d) and most importantly, a tacit agreement for the annihilation of *Canis sp.* Unlike dogs, a verbal command to a cat doesn't usually work unless it is accompanied by a look. That was something Brian had developed to a high level of sophistication while sheltering from the battleground of the Elliott household dinner table. Ebenezer III had also provided a précis of the tricks of the trade required to halt a cat in its tracks when it was considering dangling a paw in the goldfish bowl.

There was a TV advert which particularly annoyed Brian, which showed a grinning man leading a pack of dogs and cats across fields in search of an insurance policy. Communication with animals is a serious business and it's simply not good form to do it with a silly smile on your face. Then there's the fact that cats won't mix with dogs and insist on running at the front, which is the feline equivalent of travelling in business class. Dogs have their own pecking order, both within breeds and between breeds, which means it's no better than a certain no-frills airline scramble.

****

It was just after finishing his GCSEs and a month before his sixteenth birthday that Brian decided to put his skills to their ultimate test. He'd seen a recent report in the *Islington Gazette* about a mass break out of cats from a poorly run cattery on the Archway Road. He suspected this was spearheaded by a rather headstrong Abyssinian he had come across from time to time. The story hadn't attracted anything more than a ten-second spot on the local news, but it got Brian thinking about what was going on in a council flat he passed on his journeys to and from school. From listening to the barks emanating from the property he was sure there must be six dogs kept locked up in some dingy back room. The barks were high-pitched and repetitive, which is the canine equivalent of an 'SOS' call. With a plea like that there was simply no way he could continue passing by without doing something. He did try phoning the animal welfare people but they were suspicious about being phoned by someone sounding so young. Also they wanted more evidence than simple intuition. The final straw was when he told them he could understand the dogs' barking to which he was told to bugger off and stop wasting their time.

Brian spent the following weekend planning the SAS-style assault in fine detail. The first decision he made was to stage it at night when few people would be around to see a pack of animals running after him. Getting the timing right was the biggest problem as cats and dogs have no idea of time, apart from approximately when they expect to be fed. Lining them up for the taskforce involved Brian communicating something like NIGHT – OUT – WAIT the day before and then hoping they'd be ready and waiting. Cats needed some additional face-to-face communication to get them to accept the enormity of the task – plus the promise of world domination, tuna, catnip, etc.

On his way back from school Brian stocked up with treats for the dogs and tuna for the cats. He didn't have much appetite for supper and his food was argued over and eventually divided up between his brothers and sister, which suggested some sort of equanimity in the household was finally being achieved. In fact, Brian had secretly employed the latest trick he'd learnt from the Abyssinian of subduing the family with a prolonged feline stare, in the hope this would make them retire to bed early. He sneaked out of the house just after one in the morning with a rucksack on his back and wearing soft-soled shoes. He was amazed to see twelve cats and dogs all lined up to do his bidding. He couldn't help but notice the Irish wolfhound in the group who must have decided to make amends for his previous bad behaviour. They all galloped off in the direction of their target with Brian trying to stay at the head of the pack.

A previous survey of the property led Brian to believe the room where the dogs were held was towards the back of the property. Leaving his army waiting at the front of the house, Brian nervously made his way down the side passage to the small, overgrown garden. The only sound he could hear was a single, distressed, high-pitched bark coming from a room on the ground floor. Brian feared he might be too late. There was a back door with a small awning window which had been left partially open; the door was locked with a key already in place. He uttered a COME command and the cats and dogs joined him in the garden. Brian stroked the Irish wolfhound's back, weighing up the best way of getting the animals inside.

"Okay, boy, it's your turn first."

Brian went up to the door and stretched towards the window to show the dog what he wanted him to do. He used a penknife to tease open the window enough for the cats to get in. The dog came bounding towards the door and stood on his hind paws stretching up towards the window.

"Good boy! Now stay!"

Brian fixed the cats with a look and pointed at the door lock. They climbed up the Irish wolfhound's back and leapt onto the windowsill and through the awning. Brian heard scuffling noises from the other side of the door and several thuds as the cats attempted to turn the key in the lock. Suddenly the door opened. Brian stepped to the side, dreading that someone had heard the noise and come to investigate.

Success! The cats had opened the door. The dogs took their cue and streamed in, the wolfhound leading the way and immediately picking up the scent of the imprisoned dogs. A few anxious minutes later, they emerged, the wolfhound and another big dog holding malnourished dogs by the scruff of the neck and three others dragging dogs along the floor. A golden retriever managed to walk without assistance and glanced up at Brian, wagging its tail feebly. The cats brought up the rear looking pleased with themselves and expecting rewards. Brian led the motley crew to the front of the property and shone his flashlight on the dogs they had just liberated from the building. He gasped at their emaciated state. One was clearly dead, four were barely conscious and the last – the golden retriever – had just enough energy to lick his hand gratefully. He brushed away tears and reached for his mobile phone to call 999.

"Hello, this is Brian Elliott. Can you send the police, please?"

When the police arrived, they found Brian sitting against the fence looking hollow-eyed and exhausted. The cats were eating tuna off the pavement. Brian's dogs had formed a circle around the rescued dogs to keep them warm. The dead dog had been left some way away on the pavement.

"Hello, young man, are you Brian?" asked the kindly looking female police officer.

"Yes, miss," Brian replied, looking up at her with tears still in his eyes.

"Can you tell us what happened, son?" asked the male police officer.

"I rescued the dogs, except one is dead." Brian started crying again.

"That's okay, Brian," said the female officer. "Did you do that on your own, then?"

"No, they helped me," Brian replied, pointing at the cats and dogs.

"You mean *these* cats and dogs helped you?" asked the male officer incredulously.

"That's what I said," Brian replied sullenly, frustrated that no one ever seemed to believe him.

"Hmm, I think we need to get you back to your home and talk with your parents," said the female officer.

Brian said nothing.

****

The police found Brian thoroughly puzzling. His fingerprints were all over the back door and the window frame but only on the outside. Somehow the door had been unlocked from the inside and the imprisoned dogs released from an inner room. When he was prepared to talk, Brian remained adamant that the cats and dogs got into the house and freed the dogs on his instruction. No one in the custody suite wanted to put their job on the line by suggesting the animals had actually unlocked the back door. Then there were Brian's parents; his father evidently had no time for his son and his mother was in a state of emotional meltdown judging by her abundant tears. The police also found it challenging to define the precise nature of the charge; 'aiding and abetting the entry of multiple cats and dogs into said premises in order to effect the rescue of five emaciated dogs and one dog's corpse' sounded more like a recommendation for a heroism award than a justification for him to appear in front of a magistrate in a juvenile court.

Unfortunately, the occupant of the council accommodation turned out to be an acquaintance of the arresting officer and was temporarily indisposed at Her Majesty's pleasure. The officer had no intention of letting the case drop. The same police officer had also done his level best to get Brian's brother, Jason, charged with breaking and entering (times ten) and he was damned if he'd let the chance for retribution pass him by.

****

It was on a cold day in early March that found Brian back in his best clothes on a wooden bench, with his mother in floods of tears and his father pissed-off and sullen, waiting to be called before the magistrate in Islington North Juvenile Court.

The female magistrate was a kindly soul who tried to find fault with the parents before blaming the child. She surveyed the young defendant and his parents as she sat down; the evident hostility of the father viewed against the emotional outpourings of the mother confirmed her impression of a dysfunctional family. But there was obviously more happening in this case then met the eyes. The child psychiatrist's report made it clear she thought the boy was mentally ill. The magistrate wasn't so sure. The boy believed he could communicate with animals and make some respond to his commands. That assertion didn't seem quite so strange to her given the incident in the park and the subsequent TV interview. She felt somewhat implicated as it was her Irish wolfhound who'd been involved in the park incident and had also somehow entered the council property. She realised it was a conflict of interest but decided to keep that information to herself. As to why the boy had been brought before her in court, it seemed a rather trumped-up, hastily conceived bit of petty-mindedness on the part of the police. She saw no conclusive evidence he'd actually entered the premises. The end result of whatever he'd engineered was five grossly maltreated dogs receiving urgent care from the RSPCA, which sounded highly praiseworthy. But she felt something needed to be done to get him back on the right track.

"Good morning, Brian. I'm Mrs Lethbridge and I'm what's called a magistrate." She paused briefly to look at her notes. "Now the reason you're in my court today is because the police believe you were breaking and entering at–"

"I never, miss!" Brian interrupted angrily. "The police wouldn't listen! People just never believe me!"

Mrs Lethbridge looked sympathetically at Brian although she didn't like being interrupted. "Perhaps you could tell me what *did* happen, then?"

Brian looked to his father for support but he continued to stare angrily across the courtroom. His mother was still mopping away at her tears.

"It's just what I said to the police, miss."

"What did you tell them, Brian?"

"I told them I'd heard the dogs in distress when I was going to school. I phoned animal welfare but they told me to get lost. So I decided to do something about it, miss."

"What did you do, Brian?"

Brian looked shifty, not sure what to say next. "I just got some dogs and cats together, miss," he muttered softly.

"Brian, please could you speak up."

"I GOT SOME DOGS AND CATS TOGETHER!" Brian shouted.

Mrs Lethbridge noticed his parents cringing. "How did you do that, Brian?"

"I spoke to them, miss."

There was a hush in the courtroom as people took in what the young man had just said.

"Is that a bit like what happened in the park?"

"Yes, miss."

"So dogs and cats listen to you, then?"

Brian immediately brightened up; pleased someone was actually taking him seriously. He nodded.

"Except cats aren't very good at listening and need a good stare in the eyes. And they won't do anything unless I promise them four things."

"What are those, Brian?" asked the magistrate, her interest piqued.

"World domination, tuna, catnip and getting rid of dogs."

The courtroom burst into laughter.

"Are you pulling my leg, Brian?" the magistrate asked gently.

"No, miss, it's true. See, you're not believing me!"

"I believe you, Brian. Now, how did you get the dogs out of the property?"

"It was easy, really. I got the Irish wolfhound to stand on his legs, then the cats climbed up and got through the window. They opened the door, the dogs went in and got the other dogs out."

The courtroom had gone quiet again and there were a lot of shaking heads.

"And they did all that because you told them to do so?"

Brian nodded, "Yes, miss." He paused and gave the magistrate a curious look. "Your dog misses him, too, you know."

"Who's 'him', Brian?"

"Your husband, miss. That's why he's been going a bit wild recently. He's missing the top dog."

Mrs Lethbridge didn't quite know what to say. This boy… this young man clearly was rather special. She reached in her bag for a tissue and dabbed at her eyes. "Thank you, Brian. How did you know?"

"Your dog told me," Brian said softly.

There was a sudden hush in the courtroom.

Mrs Lethbridge put the tissue back in her bag. "Brian, I'm going to suggest something to you and I want you to think about it very seriously."

Brian looked her in the eyes and nodded.

"Firstly, I don't find convincing evidence you broke into the property. The dogs and cats may have done so, but they're not subject to any laws I know of."

There was a brief peal of laughter in the courtroom.

"Secondly, I believe you're a young man with a unique gift. I can't say I understand it but I believe you have it. But I'm worried it could lead you astray, as it did on this occasion. Do you understand that, Brian?"

"Yes, miss." Brian looked down at the floor.

"So, what I'm going to ask you to consider is taking on a job where you'll be surrounded by animals and with someone to keep an eye on you. What do you say to that, Brian?"

"Dunno really, miss." Brian's father nudged him hard in the ribs and he winced. "Okay, I'll try it," he said reluctantly. "Where is the job, miss?"

"It's a pet shop called Wet & Wild on Holloway Road. The owner is my nephew. I think you'll get on well there."

****

Brian had visited Wet & Wild a few times when he was younger to buy food for his goldfish. He'd been put off by the grumpy owner who always dressed in leathers, which made

Brian wonder just how many animals had been slaughtered to produce the clothing. His mother had told him the new owner was much nearer his age and had an interest in unusual animals. So, a job in the pet shop seemed worth considering, even if only to add to his haiku collection.

On entering the shop, Brian was struck by all the rich and unusual smells coming from around him and he sensed there was so much communication just waiting to happen. He saw a tank containing goldfish and darted over to examine its contents. He crouched down until his face was almost touching the glass. He didn't notice a tall man with short, dark hair coming over to speak to him.

"Hello, I'm Roderick, the owner. Are you looking for a goldfish?"

Brian waited until he'd finished communicating with the tank's emissary before responding.

"No, he's gone," he replied cryptically without turning away from the tank.

"Who was *he*?"

"Ebenezer the third. He came from the Jin Dynasty, you know."

Roderick realised this young man was the one he'd been expecting for a job interview. It was an unusual start. "You're Brian, aren't you?"

"That's right."

Brian turned slowly to look up at Roderick while still crouching in front of the tank. It was a strange, rather inquiring look and Roderick felt under scrutiny. His personas had been jostling for dominance recently and he wondered what Brian would notice. Brian suddenly smiled.

"You're different. You're not trying to be something you aren't. I'd like to work here." His eyes travelled down the length of Roderick's body. "You're a shape-shifter, aren't you?" he added as an unexpected afterthought. Roderick decided to let his observation pass without comment.

And that was the interview, one of the shortest and strangest ever. Roderick explained the cleaning and feeding duties Brian was expected to carry out every day. As they went around the various tanks and cages, Roderick noticed Brian's sparks of excitement when each animal was introduced to him. He bent down to look a large male cat in his eyes but the cat was having none of that and looked away disdainfully. But even in that briefest exchange of eye contact Brian could see the cat's fascinatingly chequered past. What with the cat and the shape-shifter owner, he was *definitely* going to enjoy working in the pet shop.

Brian was right about Roderick being a shape-shifter, too.

Chapter Two

Jeff

The pet shop was unprepossessing from the outside. It was one of a row of utilitarian shop conversions halfway down the Holloway Road in North London. The exterior had a faux panel door more suited to residential accommodation and windows which went from pavement to ceiling. Inside, there was a damp lower ground floor and a mezzanine level accessed by some wooden stairs. Other shops in the row included a travel agent, a kebab shop and a financial adviser. It also had some more prestigious neighbours, including Blackwell's Bookshop and the London Metropolitan University.

The original owner of Wet & Wild made no secret of his preference to be on the road astride his Harley-Davidson. Prior employment as a lion tamer had set the scene for his interest in creatures that purred. His aspiration to be something prodigious in big cats came to nothing and he accepted the domestic cat as second best. But his motorcycle remained his first love. With the Harley-Davidson parked outside the shop many believed Wet & Wild catered for the exotic tastes of a massage parlour and so rarely ventured behind the fogged-up windows.

Nonetheless, the business survived against all the odds, even during the double-dip recession of the 2010s. Wet & Wild's long-suffering accountant credited this to the owner's cunning knack of sourcing unusual pets that sold at a massive profit. How he found these pets remains as impenetrable as a Dickensian fog, but he did have a finger in many institutional pies through being a member of a Masonic lodge. Sadly he developed an allergy to animal fur and so he passed on the keys and intruder alarm code to a young, 'resting' actor named Roderick Jones. Roderick had been helping out at the shop and had a natural affinity for animals. The owner attributed this to his unchallenging demeanour and an animal friendly smell.

****

Roderick wasn't exactly a normal child. In fact, he was born a chimera with two sets of chromosomes. Unusually, this also extended to his nervous system, so he grew up with two brains that became individuals with their own characteristics and personalities. The young Roderick soon realised something wasn't quite right. From time to time schoolmates would see a flicker of something different and he was teased and given the nickname 'two-face'. He had no idea what was happening, of course, and retreated to the back of the class where he could be anonymous. But a drama teacher singled him out precisely because of his mutability and he found acting gave him an outlet where he was praised rather than bullied.

Somehow the twins can express themselves individually – the grey-eyed, dark-haired one and the green-eyed, blond-haired alter ego – who can manipulate those around them into seeing one or the other. This isn't exactly shape-shifting but more a mental projection by the individual jostling his position to the surface. There's also a middle ground where both individuals remain buried and Roderick becomes a nonentity; a bland figure who's immediately forgotten and can pass through life unnoticed.

Against his parents' better judgement, Roderick enrolled in drama school rather than going to university. His tutors hardly regarded him as the next Laurence Olivier but they saw a certain quality in him enabling him to blend into most casts. 'A gift for anonymity' was the way they put it. While he would never be the leading man, they said there would always be a place for him in the chorus or crowd scenes. Latterly, even this dismally paid work had dried up, and so taking on the pet shop had seemed like manna from heaven.

Roderick had also developed a curious habit of appearing to upstage more important members of the cast at moments of high drama. This was one of the hazards of being a shape-shifter with twins wanting to make their own mark on the world and not caring whether they were in front of an audience. This unpredictability had caused his septuagenarian agent to mutter, drunkenly, something about her copybook being blotted once too often and he hadn't heard from her since.

****

When Roderick first took over ownership of the pet shop two years ago, his priority had been to rationalise the stock. This included both the animals themselves and the pet-orientated accessories. The low-cost, high-volume pets, such as goldfish, kept a steady stream of income coming in, but his particular interest were the unusual pets and designer accessories appealing to discerning customers. Fortunately, the previous owner continued to keep an eye on the business and had been the source of some uncommonly rare animals.

Roderick had recently taken on an assistant named Brian – a sixteen-year-old, sallow-complexioned youth who tended to avoid eye contact with humans – to help with essential chores such as feeding and cleaning the animals. He'd interviewed him as a favour to his aunt who was a magistrate and thought some nurturing away from his dysfunctional family home might help. Roderick had been impressed by the account of his rescue of six malnourished dogs although he couldn't fathom out how he'd done it. His aunt had mentioned him having 'communication issues', which he assumed must be related to autism.

Within a few days of starting, Brian had already demonstrated a knack of calming down the occupants of the shop when it got too rowdy. He also seemed unusually interested in the tank of goldfish. Aside from the occasional contretemps with a particular cat in the shop, the arrangement was working out well, giving Roderick time to spend on public relations and drumming up business. Roderick also knew he'd want to move on at some point and he was hoping Brian would have dealt with his social unease by then. Roderick was even contemplating returning to the stage and kept his Equity membership paid up in case the right opportunity arose. He'd also started taking mime classes with a view to doing a performance somewhere that would pit the twins against each other without the distraction of speech.

****

The first day of August had been the usual slow Thursday, with no more than a single customer looking to stock up on food for his goldfish. Roderick had tried to sell him a designer goldfish bowl complete with multicolour LED mood lighting and an ultra-quiet pump, but the till remained starved of all but seventy-eight pence. At lunchtime he sat chewing a desiccated sandwich while watching Jeff, the resident electric eel, who did a sterling job keeping the lights burning in the wet part of the shop.

When the juvenile electric eel arrived a year ago, it had the unoriginal name of Eely. Roderick was a follower of long-buried progressive rock groups and he decided to rename him Jeff after Jeff Lynne, the lead singer and creative force of the Electric Light Orchestra. Although he'd never shown any musical ability apart from his sinuous dance-like movements, his beady, close-set eyes and beard-like colouring on his upper and lower jaws reminded Roderick of his namesake. The provenance of Jeff was uncertain, but he'd probably been smuggled out of the Amazon after electrocuting a baby crocodile.

The obvious claim to fame that electric eels have is their ability to produce electricity, although this is normally momentary and designed to stun other fish before they're eaten. An adult electric eel can produce a stun of five hundred volts with a current of one amp, which is enough to cause cardiac arrest in a human being. It also requires a tank of seven hundred and fifty litres capacity, which is roughly three times that of a domestic bathtub. So, caring for an electric eel is a major undertaking and on a par with large reptiles or amphibians, but with the unique bonus they can give back as well as receive. An electrical engineer devised some stainless steel plates to collect the electricity but which allowed the fish to swim around unhindered and with little impact on the viewing experience. In fact, the fish responded to this by producing regular bursts of electricity even with nothing in the tank to stun. With some electronics and a battery, Jeff became an eco-friendly power source. However, Jeff needed more than the occasional shrimp to keep the juice going and showed an interest in baby mice intended for the royal python. Roderick had a soft spot for Jeff, but even the most favoured pets in the shop need reappraisal according to supply, demand and the food bill. So the reality was Jeff would soon need to move on either to a zoo or a private collector.

The sound of the doorbell caught Roderick by surprise as he was going through the till a few minutes before his usual closing time of five. He called out, "Can I help you?" expecting a hostile retort from someone who'd drunkenly mistaken the shop door for an off-licence or the student union. He was taken aback to see a young man with spiky, blond hair wearing an expensive suit and displaying a little too much attitude for that time of day. Roderick had a quirk of matching customers with breeds of dog – a pit bull came to mind although the man also had a trace of a more exotic breed, such as a Persian greyhound.

"Yeah, mate, I'm looking for something that'll make a real statement," he said in an arrogant, estuary-twanged tone placing him right back in pit bull territory. "I've got this new penthouse pad in Clerkenwell and I want something to take centre stage in the triple height, open-plan living room. I also want a pet that'll give me something back. I'm a commodities broker, so when I invest I expect a bloody good return."

"Do you mean something companionable: a large cat or dog, for instance? Something you can stroke or play with?" Roderick asked, half wishing he'd closed the shop earlier but also seeing a welcome pound sign looming on the horizon.

"Pull the other one, mate, that's what the girlfriend is for." He chortled at his own joke and grabbed at his crotch in a pathetic imitation of Michael Jackson. "No, I want something to put on display that's shit awesome and will make people say, 'Yeah, Mikey boy, you've made it'. Something like the Hirst geezer's cow in a tank but alive rather than fuckin' dead."

Roderick almost said he didn't have anything to meet the unusual demands of the obnoxious customer, but a flicker of the lights above Jeff's tank gave him an idea. "Well, I *do* have something but he'd be quite a responsibility. Let me show you Jeff and the two of you can see what you make of one another."

Roderick motioned the customer towards Jeff's tank and the two representatives of the Amazon and the Southeast looked at each other through the glass.

"Fuck! What's that? Some sort of frigging snake?"

"No, it's an electric eel, although technically it's not an eel and belongs to the knifefish order. Its Latin name is *Electrophorus electricus*."

"What's so *electric* about it then?"

"You see the lights here?" The customer nodded. "Well, Jeff is powering the lights."

The customer's jaw dropped, disclosing way too perfect teeth. "No way! You're kidding me."

"Honestly, sir, I promise that's the truth. Electric eels produce five hundred-watt bursts of electricity to stun their prey. Some electronics top up a battery and that feeds into the shop's electricity supply."

"That's fucking amazing. I'll take it. But I'll need a bigger tank than that piddling goldfish bowl. When can you deliver?" he said without pausing for breath or indeed a second thought.

"Don't you want to know the price and how to care for it?"

"I don't care, mate. Name me a price and I'll pay double. I've got to have it."

Roderick examined the price tag attached to the tank. "Well, the price I have here is two thousand pounds which includes the tank, filter and the first month's supply of food, which we'll deliver weekly."

"I'll write a cheque for five k and that's to include a tank double the size of that one. Do we have a deal?"

Curiously, the estuary twang and expletives had vanished as soon as the financial details were wrapped up. Roderick realised further discussion about Jeff's care would be impracticable at this point as the customer was too hyped up contemplating his latest acquisition and the boost to his monstrous ego. But he was relieved the customer had spontaneously brought up the issue of a larger tank, as that's exactly what Jeff would need as he grew into adulthood. He made a few calculations on a piece of paper.

"Jeff could grow to more than two metres when he's an adult, so I reckon you'll need a tank of at least two hundred gallons. I'd recommend one made from Plexiglass; that's lighter than glass and won't crack. It's also clearer than glass, so you'll get a better view of him. If you've got the space, I suggest going for a long, narrow tank: eight feet long by two feet width and depth should be ample. How does that sound to you?"

"That's brill, mate. The bigger the better. It'll be a real babe magnet."

It was clear a two-metre electric eel and an eight-foot tank would do much for his virility. And from Roderick's monetary perspective a Plexiglass tank of that capacity would cost a lot less than three thousand pounds, so the shop would see a healthy profit from the transaction. After taking the cheque and arranging a provisional delivery date for a month's time, Roderick saw the customer to the door.

"Amazing doing business with you, mate. I'll get onto some guys I know to build a stand for the tank and sort out wiring him up to the electrics. I suppose I'll also need a crane to lift the tank into the apartment; there's a geezer I know who moves pianos and owes me a favour."

After an aggressive pump of a handshake, the customer left, whistling loudly but surprisingly tunefully. Roderick returned to the till and examined the cheque. It was hard to equate the fine handwriting and the formal 'M. Brown Esq.' with the brash individual who'd just left the shop. The account was at Coutts, which was still aspirational even if no longer limited to the upper echelons of society.

Moving Jeff from the shop into the apartment would be a challenge. His current tank should fit through the doorway and could be transported on a flatbed truck to the apartment block and then up to the penthouse. The proposed Plexiglass tank wouldn't fit into the elevator and would be easier to crane in empty rather than full of water. Moving Jeff into the new tank would take careful handling with insulated gloves, as an electric eel halfway to adulthood weighed as much as ten kilograms and was as slippery as a snake. He'd also need tiring out for a few hours to lessen the discharges to a safer level.

Roderick went back to Jeff's tank. He didn't expect to find him nearly motionless in the water with his eyes tracking his movements. Electric eels have notoriously poor eyesight, so he could scarcely have been watching him. He bent down and looked into Jeff's beady little eyes. He could have sworn he saw a glint of amusement, and when he looked at the meter next to the tank he saw Jeff's electrical output had just peaked at eight hundred watts. It was a bizarre notion, but it was almost as if Jeff was flexing his electric organs in preparation for his new owner's amusement. Roderick went to the fridge and returned with a bag of defrosted shrimps that he emptied into the tank. Jeff consumed these within seconds and returned to his previous, all but motionless state. The meter plunged in the opposite direction and it was as though Jeff was taunting Roderick to give him second helpings. Roderick smiled softly, went to the fridge and returned with another bag of shrimps. Sated, Jeff reverted to his usual sinuous circuits around the tank and the power meter responded accordingly.

Over the next two weeks, emails and texts arrived with alarming regularity demanding updates on the progress with the tank and the arrangements for the move-in day. The Plexiglass firm were doing their best to keep to the agreed delivery date despite Mikey's interference. He'd been changing his mind about the tint of Plexiglass, colour of the back panel, position of the feeding flap and filtering tubes and the lighting arrangement. Roderick eventually agreed to do a site visit to keep the customer happy and to double-check Jeff was heading somewhere suitable for his needs.

Roderick parked the Wet & Wild van outside the customer's block in one of the more gentrified parts of Clerkenwell, just off the Green. He wondered how Mikey's neighbours would react to the imminent arrival of more than two hundred gallons of water above their heads, and he prayed the renovated industrial building would support the weight. The penthouse had its own entrance and elevator which was patently designed for ferrying passengers rather than an eight-foot tank. The entry phone was answered immediately and the housekeeper greeted him as he entered the apartment. Whatever he might have originally assumed about the customer, the interior design made it clear he had excellent taste. However, he didn't expect to hear piano music drifting from the expanse of the living room with the depth and clarity of some expensive audio equipment. Roderick walked a short way across the dark wood floor and was dumbstruck to see Mikey sitting at a concert grand, playing with rapt attention and in a world of his and JS Bach's own. Roderick stood for a few moments, not wanting to disturb the tranquillity of the moment but thinking he needed to make his presence known. He coughed politely. Mikey stopped playing mid-piece and looked up, clearly taken aback by Roderick's interruption.

"Goldberg Variations?" Roderick asked semi-rhetorically. "You play really well."

"What?" said Mikey. "Yeah, well, you know, it's one of those things."

He seemed embarrassed to have a chink in his armour exposed by a stranger and put the lid down over the keys with an emphatic thud. He stood up and Roderick noticed he was barefoot. He wore faded jeans and a T-shirt, and his hair was damp and messed up as if he'd only just got out of the shower. In contrast to when he'd visited the pet shop, he appeared curiously vulnerable and appealing. Roderick realised too late he was reflexively verifying which persona he was projecting. Mikey noticed something and said, "Hey, man, what's going on there? There was some weird shit shimmering and I'd swear you looked different for a moment." He shook his head and ran his hands through his hair. "No, can't be…" He swiftly gathered his thoughts together. "No worries, man, it must be the hangover. It was some heavy drinking session last night." He extended a well-manicured hand to welcome Roderick more formally. "Welcome to my pad, mate."

Roderick shook hands and glanced around, looking for the tank. "Well, it's certainly an impressive place you've got here, but I'm wondering where Jeff will go."

Mikey chuckled. "You're right next to it, mate," he said, pointing to whatever was on Roderick's left.

Roderick looked carefully and noticed a delicate, honeycomb-like construction almost invisible against the wooden floor, despite being in the middle of the room and clearly intended to support the eight-foot tank.

"They're carbon fibre tubes," Mikey explained. "Real state-of-the-art aerospace stuff. Hundreds of translucent five mil tubes with a mesh linking them from top to bottom." He gazed adoringly at the apparatus. "And there's more…"

He reached for a panel of light switches and flicked a few on; multiple points of light shone up towards the ceiling like stars that had suddenly come into being.

Roderick's jaw dropped. "Wow! That's quite something. But are you sure it'll support the tank?"

"No problem," replied Mikey. "I've checked the calculations. And anyway I'm covered by insurance." He passed his hands over the points of light and looked up at the ceiling. "What I'm waiting to see is the silhouette of the eel against the ceiling, as if he's traversing the skies like an intergalactic mother ship."

"So less *U.S.S. Enterprise* and more something wholesomely organic?"

"Yeah, something like that. To boldly go and all that fucking sort of thing..."

He paused to reflect on his unusually philosophical musings. "Actually, mate, there is one thing I wanted to confirm, how do you think he'll react when all the LEDs are on? I mean, I don't want to piss him off or anything."

Roderick pondered for a moment. "That shouldn't be a problem. Electric eels are almost blind, so I don't think he'll notice. He might like the piano, though, as eels' hearing and sense of vibration is pretty good. But perhaps lay off the Hammerklavier to start with."

Mikey chortled, "Don't worry mate, I never touch that Beethoven shit. It's way too deep and meaningful for me. You can't beat a bit of JSB, if you ask me – particularly to clear the cobwebs in the morning. But let me show you something else."

He motioned towards the open-plan kitchen. Mikey wandered over to a row of black cupboards and pulled a handle, revealing a vast freezer compartment. "This is where I plan to store the food. There should be enough space for a good few months' worth."

Roderick nodded in agreement. "Remember to defrost the food before you feed it to him. Small fish like smelt would be even better as he grows – and live fish would encourage him to stun his prey. He's also partial to strips of raw beef."

"Sounds good to me. It's no skin off my nose sharing a steak with him, although I probably like my meat even rarer than him."

Roderick shuddered at the image. He could see his customer was someone who didn't do things by halves and would be a hell of an adversary if anything did go wrong – even if insurance covered it.

"I think that's all I need to see. It's now just a matter of finalising the moving-in logistics. I gather you've arranged for someone to lift in the new tank."

"Yeah, the guy that did the biz with the Steinway has agreed to do it half-price. But we add the water later once the eel is in the tank, right?"

"Correct," replied Roderick. "You'll need a hose to run from the kitchen sink to the tank and make sure you're wearing nonconductive gloves whenever you're doing anything with the tank. He'll pop up for air every few minutes and may also come to the surface to feed, so there's always the chance of getting a shock. Try not to make any sudden movements. Oh, and make sure the lid is always on tight."

"Okey-dokey, boss," he said with a mock salute. "I'll get the electrics sorted once the tank is in place. I'll use the eel's discharges to drive the LEDs with a sequencer, which should be bloody amazing!" His eyes lit up like a child's on Christmas morning. "And I've arranged a moving-in do – 'Sparky's Magic Party', I'm calling it – it'd be great if you could come."

Mikey led Roderick to the door and they exchanged an over-pumped handshake the way men do when asserting their dominance, although it was clear that Mikey called the shots in this business relationship. Roderick felt reassured by the visit and was almost looking forward to Jeff's moving-in do. But there were still a few items which needed tying up his end. One of these was getting Jeff a general check-up by a vet from the London Zoo who was visiting Wet & Wild later that afternoon.

When Roderick got back to the shop, he discovered someone had put up a sign in the window saying 'Special Offer on Werewolves – Full Moon Tonight'. Such strange signs weren't exactly uncommon – especially in late October – and were usually the result of Brian's latest, obsessional interest. Bizarrely, some customers believed werewolves really existed, although arguably that was no more curious than some of the exotic animals he had in store. He had a quick look at a new arrival: a Jackson's chameleon who was presently displaying colourful markings worthy of the lead role in *Joseph and the Amazing Technicolor Dreamcoat.* He also had an unusual talent Roderick hoped to capitalise on.

Just then, the doorbell rang and a friendly wave announced the vet arriving. A large, white cat sprawled on an armchair by the window looked up contemptuously and then promptly returned to pondering life, the universe and everything.

"Is that the infamous fat cat?" the vet asked.

"One and the same," replied Roderick. "I'm hoping he'll find a new home soon but his reputation does tend to precede him."

"Well at least you've got him in the right place to attract passing trade," said the vet noticing a couple of schoolchildren who were sticking out tongues and making sizeist gestures at the cat.

"That's what I'm hoping," replied Roderick, who led him to the back of the shop where Jeff's tank took pride of place.

"So, this is the young chap I've heard so much about," said the vet looking with great interest at the tank and the wires leading from it. "As you'll know, Roderick, electric eels are as rare as hens' teeth outside zoos and it's unusual to discover a juvenile with the capacity for electric discharges this fellow has. I've brought some gloves with me but I'm hoping to do the examination without putting my hands in the tank."

He leant down to get a better look at the eel. "He certainly looks healthy. Is it true he originally came from the Amazon basin?"

"That's what I gather," said Roderick. "I inherited him from the previous owner and the story went that he was smuggled out on the back of a motorcycle, although he was little more than a baby in those days."

"But I'd imagine still packing quite a punch," said the vet.

"Yes, the tale started with a baby croc getting electrocuted," explained Roderick.

"And I gather you've now got a private collector interested in him. Do you think he knows what he's letting himself in for?" the vet asked.

"I think so," replied Roderick, showing only a slight doubt. "He's not stinting on a suitable habitat and he's also got decent storage for the food. My main reservation is what he's expecting in return."

"Electricity?" the vet asked but only half seriously.

"And amusement," replied Roderick. "So, instead of dancing girls, a sinuous eel projected onto the ceiling."'

"Well, he won't be the first," said the vet. "After all, it was an aquarium which hit on the idea of using an electric eel to light up a Christmas tree. And it's probably all good PR for the cause of the electric eel."

"I suppose so," replied Roderick, "but I'll be keeping a close eye on his move-in anyway."

"Do you always provide this degree of aftercare to animals you sell?"

"Not necessarily, but Jeff is a bit special and I'll be sorry to see him go."

"I can see that – he's quite a specimen. Anyhow, I'll move on to the examination."

The vet examined Jeff through the glass from the mouth to the tip of the tail. He measured his length at a little less than one metre, which fitted with him being about five years old and halfway to full maturity. His skin looked smooth and he couldn't see any growths on the skin typical of the various parasites and bacteria that can affect fish. There'd been a report in a zoological journal of electric eels developing abdominal distension and dying if their environment was too alkaline, so he checked the pH of the tank water to make sure. The eel was swimming easily with a fluid motion from side to side, and overall there was nothing to suggest he was in anything other than rude health.

"Roderick, is it possible to see the eel feeding?"

"No problem, he's due his evening feed anyway," Roderick replied.

He went to the back of the shop where he kept Jeff's food and returned with a bag of defrosted shrimps. He put on some gloves, raised the lid and emptied the contents into the tank.

"It's good to see you're taking precautions," said the vet.

"Thanks," replied Roderick. "I've learnt the unpleasant way. A shock from Jeff is like being kicked by a mule." He grimaced.

Jeff didn't immediately alight on the shrimps. Instead, he gave a flip of his tail, shimmered his fin and then fired off a discharge, causing the output meter to peak at eight hundred watts. Satisfied he'd subdued his already dead prey, Jeff went for the kill and devoured the shrimps within seconds.

"That's one hell of an output from a juvenile eel," said the vet whose mouth had been almost as open as the eel's watching Jeff's feeding display. "And there's nothing wrong with his feeding behaviour, although I wouldn't expect him to shock food that's already dead."

He looked more closely at the equipment used to gather Jeff's discharges. "I see you're using the same idea as in Japan of plates at either end of the tank to collect the electricity."

"Yes, but we've added electronics to trickle charge a battery and then to convert the DC into mains voltage. In fact, he's currently running most of the lighting in the shop."

"That's extraordinary!" the vet said in amazement. "But how do you keep him discharging consistently enough?"

"It may sound weird but it's as if he's adapting to demand," Roderick replied, "and he doesn't tire himself out, either. The food bill has gone up massively, though."

"Well, I'm happy to give him a clean bill of health, but I wouldn't want to put him in charge of the lighting in my home," said the vet with a laugh. "I ought to get going. Do you have any other questions?"

"The other issue I wanted advice on is filtering," replied Roderick. "The filter we've got here also regulates temperature and pH. It's over-specified, so I'm hoping it'll cope with the bigger tank and avoid changes of water."

The vet inspected the filtration unit and nodded. "I think it should do the trick. The eel is relatively young and he should thrive in the larger tank. Anyhow, changing water would be asking for trouble."

****

The day came for Jeff's move into his swanky, new apartment – and his change of name, of course. Water agitators were put into the tank to stimulate him into discharging as much electricity as possible. Brian took some perverse pleasure in dangling his fingers barely above the water level in anticipation of receiving a shock or a nibble when the eel came up for air. After two hours of this, half the water was emptied so there wouldn't be too much sloshing around once Jeff was en route. It then took four of them to carry the tank out of the shop and onto the back of the flatbed truck. A sign saying 'Wet & Wild Animal In Transit – Slow Vehicle' was attached above the licence plate. Roderick sat by the tank during the snail's pace journey to Clerkenwell, keeping a close eye on the eel, the water and the tank lid. He prayed to all the animal-friendly deities he could think of that there wouldn't be an emergency stop.

Mikey was waiting for them when they arrived at 10 St John's Square. As soon as Roderick stepped down from the truck he was greeted with a high-five followed by a crushing bear hug. Although Mikey appeared wired up to the gills, he'd had the foresight to hire a motorised trolley to get the tank into the building and up into the penthouse. Mikey insisted on taking the controls of the trolley and seemed more intent on proving his aspirations to formula one racing than driving a straight and true path to the destination. When the elevator door opened to the apartment, Jeff was thoroughly shaken and stirred and his thrashing around suggested he was firing off on all cylinders.

"Er, Mikey," said an exasperated Roderick, "I think you need to calm down a bit. Jeff is getting a little overexcited which could make transferring him into the tank more difficult."

"Oops sorry, mate," replied Mikey apologetically, but still with a mischievous glint in his eyes. "It's just like all my birthdays have come at once."

Roderick noticed some white powder on the lapels of Mikey's suit jacket hinting at a premature celebration of the eel's arrival. He was about to continue the gentle scold when he caught sight of the Plexiglass tank on top of Mikey's hi-tech plinth. "Wow!" he exclaimed.

"Yeah, frigging awesome," agreed Mikey smiling broadly.

And it *was* extraordinary. In fact, Roderick could honestly say he'd never seen any fish tank anywhere looking quite like it. Now he understood why Mikey had been so insistent on confirming the tank's construction, as the plinth bonded effortlessly with the tank, giving the illusion it was floating in some dark, mysterious space. When Mikey switched the LED lights on, the tank suddenly erupted with delicate shafts of light that turned the ceiling into a dazzling starscape out of *2001: A Space Odyssey*.

Getting Jeff into the new tank dashed much of their enthusiasm, though. Having filled the new tank with a few inches of water, they used the trolley to lift the old tank until it was immediately above the new one. Gently tilting the tank down into the water should have transferred the contents from old to new. Unfortunately, Jeff proved reluctant to go with the flow and tried to hide behind the flotsam and jetsam of his previous existence amassed at the end of the tank. Without saying anything, Mikey walked across the room and sat down at the piano. As the liquid semiquavers of JS Bach's *Prelude No. 2* spread around the room, Jeff emerged from his hiding place. He looked myopically around and then eased himself into the new tank, gracefully propelling himself down the eight-foot length until he came to a full stop at the end. And there he remained while the music unfolded, his eyes seemingly watching Mikey's fingers with his fin fluttering from chin to tail like an endless ribbon of notes. At the end of the piece, Mikey stood up and walked back to the tank, bending down to take a good look at his new flatmate.

"How did you know he'd respond to that music, Mikey?" Roderick asked, thoroughly intrigued by what he'd witnessed.

"I didn't, mate," replied Mike. "It was a gut feeling. You said something about eels having good hearing and I just thought he'd like some Bach."

"As they say, 'music soothes the savage beast'," said Roderick.

"Sorry, mate, but that's misquoted," corrected Mikey gently. "The line should be 'music hath charms to soothe a savage breast, to soften rocks, or bend a knotted oak'." He tapped the glass in front of Jeff's head. "Anyhow, enough of that dead shit, let's get on with wiring up the electrics and filling the tank."

Roderick was lost for words. Mikey's fickle behaviour was irritating and fascinating in equal measure and it also painfully reminded him of his own inner conflicts.

"Hey, man, you're doing that shimmering thing again," said Mikey, rubbing his eyes in disbelief. "Fuck, that's weird. You're a strange dude all right."

"Sorry," replied Roderick, unsure what to say and trying to avoid eye contact with Mikey.

Mikey looked embarrassed. "Look, man, I didn't mean anything. You're a cool guy, really. After all, you've given me Sparky here." He looked towards the tank and then back at Roderick. "But you're still a bit weird, though."

He smiled and put his arms out to give Roderick a hug. They embraced and then drew back to look into each other's eyes. "You know, Roderick, I could get used to this – perhaps a bit of bromance or something?"

Roderick couldn't prevent himself from shimmering again and felt he was heading for end-stage persona instability. He tried to will the twins to calm down but they didn't seem to be taking notice. Mikey couldn't avoid staring. "Wow!" he said. "That's incredible!"

"Sorry again," said Roderick apologetically. "I guess I'm not that good with relationships."

"A rain check, then, until you've sorted yourself out?" Mikey suggested, smiling but a little nonplussed nonetheless.

"That's probably wise," replied Roderick, "but you could be in for a long wait."

"No problem, mate," said Mikey with a twinkle in his eyes. "You know where to find me. Meanwhile I've got old Sparky for company and I'll see you at the party anyway."

When Roderick arrived back at the shop he found the invitation to Jeff's moving-in do had arrived:

Please come to
SPARKY'S MAGIC PARTY!

8 pm Monday, 6 September
Mikey, 10 St John's Square, EC1

Bring a treat!*
*shrimps, smelt, whitebait, etc but no bones!

Roderick chuckled to himself, amused by Mikey's sense of humour. He suddenly smelt the pungently synthetic odour of cheese and onion crisps and realised Brian was looking over his shoulder.

"Is he your new boyfriend, then?" Brian asked with a smirk.

Roderick couldn't avoid blushing, which unfortunately provoked the giveaway of a shimmer.

"No, of course not," he retorted unconvincingly. "Mr Brown is the customer who bought Jeff."

"Well, I still say he's your boyfriend," said Brian with an adolescent's incontestable finality, and he walked away, singing 'I Feel Love' badly and leaving an odorous trail in his wake.

There was a time when Roderick would have sent a dog treat heading in Brian's direction after an exchange like that, but these days, he left fish to rise to the bait. And for all his maddening faults, Brian redeemed himself by treating animals with respect and patience – the one exception being Cyril the cat whose inexhaustible appetite could do battle with a black hole.

The rest of the week passed quickly enough and Roderick's focus was split between planning a mime performance at the London Mime Festival in the autumn and deciding what to put in Jeff's place. He had been offered an electric catfish but it didn't have the cachet of an electric eel and had a bad temper to boot. It was also even uglier than Jeff. So, for the time being, Frank the chameleon was in the limelight, and Brian had set up a platform in his cage with a camera so customers could watch him on a flat screen TV. Unfortunately, Cyril wasn't keen on this upstaging and whenever he ventured from his armchair it was usually to cast hissy aspersions on this pretender to the throne.

****

As Roderick pressed the elevator button to go up to the penthouse, he found himself running through all the pros and cons of attending Jeff's moving-in do. Top of the list suggesting he should immediately press the stop button was the alarming destabilisation of his defences in the presence of Mikey. However, he reckoned there'd be safety in numbers, particularly if the attention was on Jeff rather than himself. Anyway, he owed it to Jeff to be there and he'd brought along some succulent tiger prawns as a treat.

As the elevator door opened, it was clear Mikey had gone for the kill with his party planning. Attractive waiting staff almost outnumbered the guests and champagne and canapés were flowing freely. The host wandered over to him.

"Great that you're here, mate," said Mikey who was clad in black and clearly relishing being on the crest of a wave.

"I've got some tiger prawns for J... I mean, Sparky," Roderick said, briskly correcting himself and feeling a bit out of place amid all the glamour.

"Brill, let's go and feed him," said Mikey who put an expensively Rolexed hand on Roderick's shoulder and led him over to the tank.

Although Roderick had already seen the tank in daylight, he'd underestimated the impact of seeing the whole kit and caboodle at night time. Rather than merely being a fish in a tank – admittedly a large one – Mikey had transformed the humdrum into an art installation worthy of Tate Modern. Roderick craned his neck to watch the spectacle on the ceiling, and observed the eel tracing a meandering passage through the twinkling star-field.

"Amazing, simply amazing," Roderick said eventually. "How did you get the lights to flash like that?"

"Ah, that's the sequencer," replied Mikey beaming with pleasure. "The low voltages Sparky produces trigger a box which cycles the LEDs in turn and the big discharges show up on the display." He pointed to the opposite wall where there was a huge '800' projected in red.

"It's like something Gene Rodenberry might have dreamt up; the space creature lost among the stars looking for its soul mate."

Mikey looked delighted. "That's exactly it!"

Sparky already had many admirers who were busy taking shots with mobile phones and lining up to pass treats through the feeding flap. Roderick also noticed a small posse of photographers waiting to pounce on guests and he could well imagine the party appearing on the glossy pages of *Hello* magazine.

"He's a beauty, isn't he?" said a man to his left, who was dark-skinned, dramatically tall and, like Mikey, wearing black.

"Yes," agreed Roderick. "I was sorry to see him go, but he was getting too big."

The man looked taken aback. "Are you the guy who Mikey bought the electric eel from?"

"That's me. I'm Roderick." They shook hands. "And you are?"

"I'm Markus, otherwise known as DJ Mista Mixa for my sins."

"A DJ?" Roderick said with partial disbelief. "So, how do you know Mikey?"

"Well, we both studied piano at the Royal Academy of Music," replied Markus with the tired smile of someone who'd given the explanation many times that evening.

"You're kidding!" Roderick exclaimed with a look of utter incredulity.

"Honestly, it's true, but it was always Mikey who won the prizes."

"I'm impressed. So neither of you was cut out for the concert platform?"

"Definitely not. Turntables and a mixing desk are more my thing, although perfect pitch and sense of rhythm are very handy when you're dropping tracks. But Mikey could have gone all the way."

"What happened then?"

"Oh, numbers got in the way. Mikey was always trying to find the hidden meaning in music and believed number theory was the answer to everything. Now it's something called 'commodities' which has his attention and it's certainly making him a fortune – as you can see."

"And what about the machismo and wandering accent?"

Markus laughed. "Oh, he's taken a leaf out of a certain punk-haired violinist's book."

"I guessed it was something like that," Roderick smiled. "You know, Markus, I've got a pet in the shop which might suit you rather well."

Roderick offered him his business card. "My shop is on the Holloway Road, so drop by and I'll show you young Frank."

Just then, the two of them noticed Mikey crossing the floor to the piano. He touched the screen on his iPhone and the music stopped. All conversation in the room subsided and the guests turned towards Mikey in expectation of a speech. "This is for you, Sparky," he said softly, sitting down at the keyboard. Mikey started playing the last and most enigmatic piece from Bach's *Art of Fugue*. Right from the serene opening bars, Mikey had the rapt attention of the entire room, barely daring to breathe lest they disturb the ebb and flow of the counterpoint. The lines gave the impression of eels sinuously entwining with one another. At the point where the unfinished score broke off, Mikey added in the fourth part of the fugue, extemporising as if Johann Sebastian himself was at the piano. Roderick looked across at the tank and saw that Sparky was as spellbound as everyone else. As the final D major chord died away, the power display hit nine hundred watts, almost as if Sparky was giving him a standing ovation. Mikey stood up from the piano, said, "Welcome, Sparky mate," and swallowed the contents of the champagne flute in one.

"Okay, let's party!" Mikey announced to the stunned throng.

Roderick looked at the other guests. Some were brushing away tears and that included DJ Mista Mixa who seemed more affected than most. Roderick wondered whether he and Mikey had shared more than the colour of their clothes at some point in the past. He noticed them exchanging a lingering embrace that hinted as such. Roderick took the opportunity to leave. The emotional yearning of Bach's final masterpiece had left him drained and further social interaction with other guests simply wasn't wise in that condition.

****

Mikey could have dined for years on the publicity from the party. Fashion shoots competed for the prestige of renting the space but Mikey was reticent about allowing invasion of their privacy. But eventually he gave in, and a film crew and all its parasitic sycophants were parked almost daily outside 10 St John's Square. Bit by bit, Mikey got bored with the tedium of caring for Sparky and passed on the daytime feeding to his housekeeper. Sadly, her phobia of snakes prevented her from performing this duty and so much of Sparky's food ended up going down the waste-disposal unit. Outwardly, Sparky didn't seem much different, but someone paying him more attention would have noticed the lights were dimmer and his movements were those of an animal searching for something.

Mikey returned from his unusually scheduled, Saturday business meeting feeling pumped up and ready to hit a club or two once he'd had a shower. He didn't expect to see lights on in the apartment and guessed the automation system had switched them on. Alternatively, he might have pressed the wrong icon on his iPhone. He inspected himself in the mirrored elevator walls and preened. "Shit!" he exclaimed to the mirror after noticing his roots were showing. As the elevator neared his apartment he heard loud music coming from inside. Could be the automation again, he concluded, although perhaps it was his girlfriend choosing to surprise him.

When the elevator door opened, the wall of sound nearly knocked him off his feet. Techno at over one hundred decibels was acceptable in a club but not in his home. And the lights had gone out. His flicked some switches but no lights came on.

"What the fuck are you playing at, Charlie?" he ineffectually shouted into the thumping darkness of the living room. Suddenly the sound stopped, leaving a strange vacuum of silence. "Okay, very clever, Charlie, but switch the bloody lights back on, will you?"

He walked across the polished wooden floor that showed reflections from the streetlights outside. Strangely, the surface of the floor was shimmering like oil. He took another step forward and felt the leather sole of his right shoe sliding uncontrollably forward. He put his left hand out to grab at any support and a floor lamp came crashing down. Mikey was the next to fall to the floor. His left hand felt the coldness of water on the floor. His outstretched right hand felt something different: indisputably neither wood nor water but something slightly warm and very slimy. There was some movement to his left. He turned his head and saw Sparky's beady little eyes examining him from a scant few inches away. He felt a tingling in his fingers and then Sparky's bolt of electricity hit him and he lapsed into unconsciousness, vaguely aware the same techno track was blaring away again. And why had the stars come out suddenly?

The call came into the police control room at two on the Sunday morning when most of Clerkenwell was tucked up in their beds, expecting a lie-in and then a leisurely brunch in one of the many neighbourhood cafés. Those in and around the building that was 10 St John's Square had long since abandoned expectations of a quiet night and a day of rest. The content of the call was innocuous enough and common at a weekend: some idiot playing music too loudly, so please could someone read him the riot act. But more calls followed: strange problems with PCs and other electrical equipment suffering power surges, flashing lights at the top of the building and water cascading into the floors below the penthouse at number 10. Neighbours of the occupant of the penthouse had tried to contact him but the landline and mobile phone weren't answered. Plainly someone had switched the music and lights on in the first place, so it was possible the occupant wasn't currently in a position to switch them off. Speculation was rife and running at the top of the agenda was a drug overdose.

When the two police officers arrived outside 10 St John's Square, twenty or so onlookers had gathered outside. Some were wearing dressing gowns over nightclothes; others were voyeuristic passers-by intrigued by whatever was going on in the penthouse. And it certainly was a breath-taking spectacle worthy of Jean Michel Jarre at his most flamboyant. Hundreds of otherworldly dots of light danced to coruscating arpeggios and blistering orchestral stabs, with a hypnotic, driving bass line underneath.

It was also irritating for those trying to sleep and unquestionably represented a breach of the peace. So the police officers had no hesitation about their course of action. Gaining access proved problematic, as there was no response to the entry phone for number 10. Luckily, one of Mikey's neighbours – in fact, the one whose apartment had been flooded – had front door keys, but they then discovered the elevator was out of order. In the days when the building was used for industrial purposes, there'd been a fire exit from the fourth floor but Mikey had blocked it off. That left the fire brigade and their extendable ladder as the only means of access. Fortunately, one of the windows had been left half open, so breaking and entering probably wouldn't be necessary.

The fire engine arrived an hour after the initial call to the police. Meanwhile, the number of onlookers had expanded to about forty and some entrepreneur had arrived on the scene with a mobile coffee and hot dog stand and was doing a roaring trade. Extending the aerial platform ladder and getting two fire officers up into the penthouse took but minutes. It was fortunate they were wearing rubber-soled boots.

The two fire officers gingerly stepped through the open window and put their feet in the water covering the floor. They looked around, trying to take in everything. They could see a large fish tank, illuminated from underneath, but it seemed empty. The deafening music was coming from all around and they couldn't see a control panel to switch it off. To the right of where they'd entered, there was a grand piano, the ebony keys shining in the moonlight like the teeth of some ebony-skinned Leviathan.

"Jesus! What the hell was that?" exclaimed one of fire officers who'd cast his torch beam over the floor near the window. "I'd swear something moved."

He moved the light further into the corner and saw an outstretched hand. "Christ, there's a body here! You'd better get the paramedics up here pronto." He took his gloves off and bent down to examine for a pulse. The next thing he knew some massive force had sent him flying backwards against the legs of the piano.

"Fuck!" said the other fire officer, reaching for his radio. "We've got one man down – hit by an unknown assailant and probably concussed – and also a body – male, dressed in a suit and either dead or unconscious. Request backup and paramedics ASAP."

Wary of moving from where he stood, he combed the expanse of the living room with the light from the torch. And that's when the subject of his worst nightmare appeared: a four-foot long snake wiggling towards his feet. He stood frozen to the spot, unable to breathe and waiting for the serpent to strike.

Fortunately the fire officer's backup didn't have such an aversion to snakelike creatures. He speedily established that the 'serpent' was an electric eel that had escaped together with much of the water. The paramedics ascertained that the body in the suit was alive, although his breathing was shallow and his heart rate was slow. He was removed from the watery scene post-haste and returned to the ground for transfer as a blue light call to the nearest emergency department.

A fire officer found the circuit breakers and was finally able to end the onslaught on their eardrums. Their next task was to render the scene safe by removing the source of further potential electrocution, although Sparky proved to be a slippery customer. In the end, they managed to improvise a fishing net out of wooden poles and an old safety net they'd found in a locker on the fire engine. Sparky was placed in the bathtub with enough water to keep him alive but not so much that he could escape again. Various wooden bath mats were commandeered as lids to further limit his freedom. Someone also had the presence of mind to feed him a few bags of shrimps they found already defrosted in the fridge.

The clearing up was commenced once daybreak arrived. With Sparky no longer at large and most of the water sucked up, the electricity supply to the building was restored and the elevator was finally operating. A team arrived from the London Zoo to take charge of Sparky. With the help of some more shrimps he was persuaded to wiggle his way into a five-foot Perspex tube, which they used as an electric eel carrier.

****

As soon as Roderick heard about the St John's Square incident come Monday morning, he asked Brian to take charge of the shop and headed for the hospital to check on the unfortunate Mikey. This was more a damage limitation exercise than a friendly visit and he was trying to reassure himself he hadn't omitted anything before selling the electric eel. He had a brief panic when he remembered 'The Dangerous Wild Animals Act 1976' and was relieved to see that *Electrophorus electricus* wasn't on the list. When he arrived at the hospital, he had another momentary scare when the receptionist said, "Oh yes, I think he was admitted to critical care, but let me find out for you."

As Roderick discovered a minute later, Mikey had been admitted to the critical care unit but he was then transferred to the medical assessment ward. And he assuredly wasn't at death's door.

Roderick wasn't entirely sure what to expect but anticipated Mikey would be back to his usual spiked-up and acerbic self. So it came as a shock when he saw him dozing peacefully in his bed, with his hair flattened and a cherubic smile on his face. Roderick sat down by the side of the bed and touched Mikey gently on the arm.

"Oh, hello, Roderick," he said politely and without a trace of estuarial inflection. "Thanks for coming to see me. You heard what happened, then?"

"The bare bones, Mikey," Roderick replied. "Christ, I was so worried when they told me you were in critical care."

"Actually, it's Michael. I can't imagine why I wanted to be called Mikey." He seemed pensive. "It was all my fault, of course. I wasn't looking after Sparky properly and I suppose he went looking for food. I don't blame him, really; I'm sure

I'd have done the same. It's weird, Roderick, but somehow the business with Sparky has made me realise I need to stop pretending. I've decided to sell the apartment, quit the job, move somewhere quiet and concentrate on music."

"Not techno and other clubby stuff, then?"

"Goodness no." He looked aghast. "I mean JS Bach. I'm thinking of writing a book on his keyboard works." He paused. "So what will happen to Sparky?"

"The London Zoo have taken him – he'll be quite a feather in their cap."

"That's good. I'll have to visit him sometime."

"I suppose you'll be wanting your money back?" Roderick asked nervously.

"Oh no. I've had my money's-worth and it's only right he moves somewhere that can look after him properly."

"I appreciate that, Michael. To be honest, I was dreading how you'd react."

He smiled, "You mean, how Mikey would have reacted?"

"Well, he did have a habit of getting his own way."

"Yes, I suppose I did but that's all over now."

They looked into each other's eyes. Michael's piercing gaze stripped back layers to the reality underneath. Roderick realised he was shimmering but did nothing to stop it. He brushed Michael's cheek with his fingertips. A sigh escaped Michael's mouth.

"Sorry," said Roderick, embarrassed and shimmering redly.

"You don't have to be," said Michael softly. "It's just been a long time since–"

"–Markus?"

"You guessed?"

"Well, you do dress the same."

"It sounds corny but we met playing piano duets. He was the first and last. A lot's changed since then."

"You know, when you came into the shop that first day I didn't like you."

"Too much attitude?"

"And the accent."

"Then it's my turn to be sorry."

"You don't have to be."

"Thanks."

A phlebotomist arrived to take some blood samples. "I'd better be on my way, then," said Roderick. "So, bromance or something?"

"Definitely something, but give me time," replied Michael. "I'll let you know when I've moved."

Roderick bent down and gently kissed Michael on the lips. As Roderick left Michael's bedside, the phlebotomist was left wondering what was happening to her vision, as her patient's visitor was shimmering before her eyes.

****

The police, fire brigade and insurance company made a comprehensive incident report between them. They also received input from the doctors who treated Mikey in the hospital plus specialist advice from the London Zoo who'd successfully rehoused Sparky in a more appropriate habitat. They speculated the eel became agitated and aggressive because it wasn't fed regularly. Discharges from the angry eel caused power surges which a) caused havoc with Mikey's home automation system, including the audio and lighting controls, and b) led to a burnout in the filtration pump which then melted and leaked the contents of the tank onto the wooden floor and into the apartment downstairs. The lid to the tank probably wasn't fastened securely which allowed the eel to escape from the tank and slither down the side onto the wet floor. It was then that Mikey returned to the apartment, slipped on the wet floor and was shocked – probably repeatedly – by his pet. Mikey's transformation from wide boy to gentle aesthete was attributed to the electric shocks, which were thought to have treated an undiagnosed mood disorder.

****

Roderick looked at the envelope on his desk. It was made from a thick, high-quality paper that his mother used to refer to as 'Basildon Bond'. She regarded this as the gold standard for communication in the days when people still bothered writing to each other. More unusually, the envelope was handwritten in italics with a fountain pen. Intrigued, Roderick opened the envelope as neatly as he could and took out a carefully folded sheet of paper with the same italic writing. He read:

Dear Roderick,

Well, I've moved out of 10 St John's Square. It's not a large place but there's room for the piano and me. It's also not exactly the countryside – Highgate Village, in fact! – but I've got a view of greenery from my desk and there are no neighbours to worry about.

I've told Markus to visit the shop. He'd be good for you.

Very best wishes,

Michael (FKA Mikey)

Chapter Three

Cyril

Cyril was quite probably the fattest cat known to veterinary science. A succession of vets specialising in, ironically, small animals had drawn a blank on reducing his vast bulk, which spread across his favourite cushion like Jabba the Hutt from *Star Wars*. When he first arrived in the shop he'd tipped, and almost broken, the scales at fifteen kilograms. His most disarming characteristic was a Cheshire cat grin, which was due to the ample flesh of his face finally succumbing to gravity.

Cyril had found his way into the pet shop circuitously following rejection by Battersea Dogs & Cats Home on account of his size and insatiable appetite. His previous owner had been an elderly woman living in a sprawling Victorian house with only Cyril for company. One day last December, the courier delivering his weekly supply of food had been unable to get a reply when he tugged on the ancient bell pull and so he'd left the food on the doorstep. This eventually prompted neighbours to investigate the breakdown of the usual routine and they'd found themselves overwhelmed by the inexplicable feeling that somebody or something inside the house was desperate for food. Fearing the worst, they phoned the police who broke down the front door. The scene that greeted them was both tragic and bizarre. Sprawled on the living room floor was an emaciated, elderly woman in a flimsy nightdress with her hands outstretched as if summoning the last vestiges of strength to answer the doorbell. A few feet away from her, a large white cat sat on a richly upholstered footstool, its small, weirdly grinning face poking up amid the spreading hillock of fur and flesh. It was purring contentedly, the vibrations resonating around the sparsely furnished room. The red stains around the cat's mouth indicated he'd been eating recently but it obviously hadn't been his usual couriered diet. The elderly woman was admitted to hospital and the damage caused to her by the cat was easily treated. Sadly, her malnourishment was so severe that she succumbed to pneumonia and died a week later.

Cyril, on the other hand, was in a much healthier state and had no problems adapting to the routine of the pet shop. Roderick had no particular expectation of a quick sale and was happy to give him pride of place on an armchair to the right of the front door. Someone had attached a label saying 'Cyril's chair' to make it clear he wouldn't take kindly to any interloper looking for somewhere to sit.

Brian had also set up a cat cam so anyone connecting to the shop's website could eavesdrop on Cyril's activities. These usually amounted to sleeping, eating and grooming plus the occasional feline fart. It didn't take long for Roderick to discover Cyril's unusual talent. Unlike 99.999 per cent of other examples of *Felis catus*, Cyril didn't miaow incessantly when he wanted feeding. Instead he possessed the curious ability to make his need known by somehow getting inside the head of whoever was expected to feed him. Roderick mentioned this once to a vet but the disbelief with which this assertion was greeted was a sure sign to change the topic, unless he wanted to find himself in the mental health cubicle of the nearest hospital's emergency department.

Every morning when Roderick unlocked the front door to the shop and switched off the intruder alarm, he'd experience a feeling cajoling its way into his brain. He learnt this was Cyril wanting his feeding bowl filled: a sort of 'I am hungry' message wrapped up in a big, warm hug. But as Roderick discovered one cold January morning when the door lock froze, Cyril's feral nature was only just beneath the surface of his domesticity. Any delay in his feeding was unwise; having one's nervous system torn to shreds by his claw-like, 'I am angry' feelings wasn't an experience to be repeated. This meant anyone brave enough to take on Cyril's board and lodging needed to be able to assure continuity. A few brave souls took on Cyril for a probationary period, but it wasn't long before he was back in the shop spread out on his cushion.

Roderick looked up from his laptop and glanced fondly at Cyril. The cat had recently achieved celebrity status after Brian posted a video from the cat cam on YouTube that he'd set to Donna Summers' 'I Feel Love'. The video ended with Cyril languorously licking what remained of his genitalia and grinning at the camera, which perfectly summed up a cat's inclination to self-love. Cyril was now getting a steady stream of presents through the mail as well as occasional visitors bearing titbits. One woman in particular appeared enamoured of his ample charms. In fact, she bore a passing likeness to him, as she was of similar proportions, with a small but pleasant face above a vast body enveloped by a white, tent-like smock over white leggings. She was currently bending over Cyril, tickling his jowls and making babyish cooing noises. He was purring contentedly and viewing her through half-closed, limpid green eyes.

"Gee, Mr Jones, I hope you don't mind me spending so much time with Cyril," Sara Jane called out from across the shop. "He's such a cutie."

"You're welcome," replied Roderick. "He obviously likes your company. In fact you could continue stroking him all day and he'd still want more. He's a greedy old thing." He looked across at Cyril's armchair: white fur and smock blended into one. "From your accent, I'm presuming you must be from the USA."

"Actually, I'm Canadian but everyone makes that mistake. I did spend some years in San Francisco and I imagine the Bay Area accent rubbed off on me. In fact I lived on Macondray Lane in Russian Hill, which was recast as 28 Barbary Lane in *Tales of the City*."

"Great books, but Anna Madrigal didn't come across as a cat person. She seemed more interested in tending to human waifs and strays plus the occasional cannabis plant."

Sara Jane laughed. "That's true, but I think we share something which makes us more simpatico than most. You know, a sort of capacity to share with others." She stroked

Cyril's head tenderly. "It might sound strange but it's as if Cyril is trying to tell me something. I get this strange feeling in my head. It's not far off being a thought but I can't fathom the words. It's weird but also rather nice and makes me feel warm inside." She looked embarrassed.

"Sara Jane, I think you've been Cyriled," said Roderick.

"Cyriled?" She looked puzzled.

"It's like being Tangoed, except it's a wash of cat emotions rather than a sugary, orange drink," explained Roderick.

"Wow, that's exactly what it's like!" Sara Jane exclaimed. "How do you know?"

"I've been Cyriled as well. In fact it happens regularly as clockwork, twice a day, whenever he's due his food."

"How does he do it?" asked Sara Jane.

"I've no idea. I suppose it's a sort of cat ESP, although I've learnt it's not a good idea to let on that I think a cat is talking to me."

"I guess not. Next stop, loony tunes. So is it always a nice feeling you get from him?"

"Not exactly," replied Roderick scratching his head. "If he doesn't get his food on time he can get a bit nasty."

"What's that like?"

"A bit like a cat scratching around in your brain. Not very pleasant. So I make sure I always feed him on time."

"Well, I still think he's cute." She looked down at Cyril. "Is he really for sale?"

"Oh yes, he's definitely for sale, but I usually suggest a trial period because he's so much to take on."

"You mean his size and appetite?"

"And getting inside your head."

"Have others tried before?"

"Yes, and going on holiday was usually the final straw in the relationship."

"Cyril objected?"

"Strongly."

"Well, I don't usually go on holidays, so that wouldn't be a problem. And there's already a dog flap in the kitchen door, so he should be able to fit through it."

"What work do you do?"

"I'm a website designer, so I work from home. And I live around the corner in case I ever need your help."

"Well, I guess it could be a match made in heaven, but I'd still suggest a trial period in case it all goes pear-shaped."

"More pear-shaped than me?"

"Sorry, I didn't mean..." Roderick looked embarrassed.

"I know, honey. I think Cyril and I will get on absolutely fine. I'm happy to put down the dollars right now. Will you throw in the cushion?" She handed Roderick her credit card.

"Cyril wouldn't have it any other way. It's part of his fixtures and fittings. You can take his feeding bowl as well. Do you want to borrow a cat carrier?"

She looked reflective as if remembering something. "I had a kitty as a child that I used to take for walks. Do you think Cyril would walk home with me?"

Roderick looked at Cyril who was taking an unusually close interest in the conversation and had stopped grooming mid-cycle to prick up his ears and watch them. "Well, he's got some Maine Coon and a bit of Savannah in him, and he's been on a leash before, but you'll need to gain his trust first. A good start would be to give him a treat before you attach the leash to his collar."

Roderick passed Sara Jane a leash from an adjacent display. Cyril didn't react and continued to look at them quizzically through the slits of his aqua-green eyes. Sara Jane offered him a mouse-shaped treat that he took from her hand.

"Well, that's an encouraging sign," Roderick said. "He won't normally eat anything unless it's in his bowl. He's a stickler for mealtime etiquette."

Sara Jane tickled Cyril under his jaw. Roderick saw her face morphing into a catlike expression of pleasure with her eyes half-closed. "Ooh, he just gave me a big, warm hug. I think he was saying he likes me."

Cyril certainly had the knack of knowing who was a soft touch. Sara Jane attached the leash to Cyril's collar and gently coaxed him off his cushion. "Okay, cutie pie, you and I are going for a little walk to your new home. Say goodbye to Roderick."

Cyril slowly turned his head to look at Roderick. He was grinning wider than usual and Roderick could have sworn Cyril gave him a knowing wink. Roderick handed back Sara Jane's credit card and added Cyril's cushion to a carrier bag containing the feeding bowl and a starter pack of cat food. "He likes dry food best and there's enough there for about a week. Try to limit his food to about fifty grams twice a day although he'll do his best to persuade you to give him more. You can always order it online and have it delivered."

"Thanks. I'll arrange that as soon as we get home." Sara Jane turned to Cyril whose twitching whiskers suggested he was ready to investigate the outside world. Roderick opened the door for the two of them and they barely squeezed through, with Cyril leading the way.

"Call if you have any problems with Cyril settling in," said Roderick. "Our after-sales service is second to none," he added with a smile.

"Thanks, Roderick. I'll be sure to call."

Roderick watched as Sara Jane and Cyril wobbled their way down the road, their ample backsides swinging from side to side in remarkable synchrony. It was a curious but touching sight and surely one which belonged in an Armistead Maupin novel. He went back into the shop and wrote 'Gone on vacation' on a card, which he placed on Cyril's chair.

Sara Jane and Cyril attracted plenty of glances and smiles as they walked along. Someone pointed from the other side of the road and shouted, "Look at the fat pussies!" Neither human nor cat reacted and continued their perambulation. Cyril was pulling on the leash and his raised ears and sniffing suggested he was anticipating something interesting ahead. They turned the corner and a young man with intense blue eyes and artfully ripped T-shirt and jeans neared them, walking a Chihuahua dwarfed by Cyril's bulk. The dog yapped aggressively and

Cyril responded by raising his hair and unleashing a hiss worthy of Hades, which sent the dog scurrying behind its owner's trainers, its skinny tail drooped between its spindly legs.

"Cat one, dog zero," said the young man, with a friendly smile. He leant forward and gave Sara Jane a peck on the cheek. "That sure is some cat you've got there, Sara Jane."

"Cyril meet Pete, Pete meet Cyril," said Sara Jane gazing warmly at her new feline acquisition. The young man bent down to stroke Cyril's head and was met with a suspicious stare through the slits of his eyes and then a studied sniff.

"We've come from the pet shop," Sara Jane explained. "Cyril and I are kindred spirits. It was love at first sight."

That obviously wasn't the case for Cyril and the Chihuahua, and they continued their Mexican standoff.

"How come you're on your own today?" Sara Jane asked.

"Oh, Sam's in a huff because I didn't fancy sex this morning," replied Pete. "I said I was ovulating but he didn't think that was funny. So, Mr Choo and I are out for walkies on our own. Perhaps we ought to meet up for a cat/dog rematch when Sam and I are on speaking terms again."

"Sounds good. Drop round whenever you feel like it. I'll need a break from the website design I'm doing for a company selling incontinence products."

"Yuck," replied Pete. "Rather you than me." He looked at Cyril who was pulling on the leash. "Your cat's letting you know he's bored. I'll see you soon, Sara Jane."

"Bye, Pete, and give my love to Sam when you're talking again."

Sara Jane and Cyril crossed the road and stopped in front of the steps going down to her basement apartment. "Welcome to my humble abode, Cyril. Would you care to go first?" Cyril turned his head towards Sara, sniffed the air and started walking confidently down the steps.

"Wait for me," Sara Jane called, struggling to hold on to the leash and the carrier bag at the same time as rummaging for her house keys.

Cyril paused at the bottom of the steps to sniff the earth in a plant pot and rubbed the side of his head against the coarse stem of the plant. He looked up at Sara Jane as if to say, "Yes, this will do."

Sara Jane unlocked the door and the two of them crossed the threshold. Cyril sniffed his way around the living room, smelling for evidence of previous animal inhabitants. Reassured, he stopped near an armchair, making it clear where he wanted to sit. "You've got excellent taste, Cyril," Sara Jane said. "That's my favourite chair, too, but since you're the guest, you're welcome to call it your own."

She extracted the cushion from the bag, brushed off some hairs and arranged it on the chair. Cyril jumped up, spread himself generously across the cushion and purred happily. Cyril looked up at Sara Jane and she became aware of a warm, content feeling spreading itself across her consciousness. "I don't know how you do that, Cyril, but I think it's perfectly fine and dandy. Now you be good while I go order some more food for you."

Sara Jane walked across to an alcove near the kitchen where she had her computer and work area. It didn't take her long to find a source for Cyril's food and she placed a recurring monthly order, with the first delivery in a few days' time. She felt Cyril's warm hug again but this time it was with a feeling only too identifiable as hunger. She recalled what Roderick said about him scratching around if he didn't get what he wanted, so she didn't delay pouring a handful of nuggets into his bowl. Cyril jumped down from the chair with surprising grace and made a beeline for the bowl, devouring the contents with barely a pause for breath. Cyril looked up expectantly and she suddenly felt a visceral sense of hunger with an intensity that frightened her. She reached for the bag of cat food and poured him another small portion. Leaving him to eat, she went to the kitchen and prepared herself a mound of peanut butter and jelly sandwiches using sourdough bread she'd baked the previous day. Sara Jane returned to the sitting room to eat her food and saw that Cyril was back on his cushion, eyes closed, enjoying a postprandial nap.

Later that afternoon, Sara Jane found herself struggling with HTML code to display male incontinence pads in their full glory while retaining propriety. She felt something insistently rubbing against her legs and jumped. She'd momentarily forgotten she had a new flatmate. "Well, Cyril, what can I do for you? Do you want to see the rest of the apartment?" His ears pricked up expectantly as she was talking to him and his whiskers twitched inquisitively. "Okay, I'll take that as a yes."

The two of them went from room to room, Cyril sniffing and inspecting features that smelt or looked interesting. The bathroom was the least intriguing to him, as it was all too clean and clinical with an off-putting citrus smell emanating from the toilet. He found Sara Jane's bedroom much more interesting and spent minutes rolling around on the duvet before ending on his back with paws in the air, waiting for a belly rub. Sara Jane figured this was all part of him settling in and bent down to stroke his stomach. As she did so, she felt Cyril using the big, warm hug, although this time it extended beyond the confines of her head into a glow that spread throughout her body. She caught her breath and felt her cheeks flushing. This is truly bizarre, she thought. Here I am stroking a cat and I'm experiencing a feeling I haven't had since I was a teenager. She looked down at Cyril who was still stretched out on the bed like an overfed Casanova in a fur coat. She reached for a corner of the duvet and gave it a forceful yank, obligating Cyril to turn over rather ungraciously, like righting a capsized cruise ship. Cyril half-jumped, half-fell onto the bedroom floor with a resounding thump and looked up at her with the expression of one who's been slighted.

"Okay, Cyril, this is my private space and I don't want you in here 'cos you'll get the bed linen covered in fur. Capice?" Cyril sidled out of the bedroom with his tail held imperiously high, his belly slung low and almost touching the floor. He glanced back at Sara Jane as if to retort, in true Schwarzenegger style, "I'll be back."

The next stop in Cyril's guided tour was the kitchen, and most importantly, the cat flap. Sara Jane wasn't sure how to get a cat used to a cat flap but reasoned Cyril must have experienced a pet door or two in his past. True, the pet door in her apartment was designed for a dog rather than a large cat, but she doubted Cyril would notice any difference. Cyril walked slowly around the kitchen, sniffing, inspecting the floor and rubbing against corners of cupboards. He found a splodge of peanut butter and jelly on the floor and consumed this with relish. Sara Jane knelt down next to the cat flap and pushed it open with a finger, encouraging Cyril to explore what was on the other side. Seemingly disinterested, Cyril continued his forensic examination of the kitchen floor, hoping to discover other morsels which had fallen from his mistress's food plates. Sara Jane retrieved the food bowl from the living room, added a few nuggets of cat food and passed it through the cat flap onto the ground outside. She held the flap open so Cyril could smell the food. He ambled up to the door, examined the flap for cat odour and then squeezed his bulk through the opening. Sara Jane moved the food bowl back into the kitchen and Cyril eventually came back through the flap in search of his food after a slow mosey around the recycling bin. Satisfied Cyril was reacquainted with cat flap technique, Sara Jane returned to her desk and her current concerns with making male incontinence appear user-friendly.

****

Over the next few weeks, Sara Jane and Cyril were regularly seen ambling along the streets near Holloway Road and in the local park. A cat on a leash was a novelty, of course, but Cyril's size made him appear more doglike than catlike when seen at a distance. Closer up, there was no doubt about his species. Somehow the odd couple of a cat on a leash and owner looked no more unusual than a man with a buzz cut walking a Rottweiler, and a hundred times less threatening. Sara Jane's acquaintances were also delighted to see her out and about and benefiting from the exercise. That included Roderick Jones, who was out with a dog for his morning constitutional.

"Hi, Sara Jane!" Roderick called out.

Sara Jane glanced towards the voice and saw a tall man with long, blond hair walking a dog with a shaggy, golden coat. She waved at him, not entirely sure who she was waving at. As she and Cyril got closer, his features and even his hair colour had changed and she realised he was the owner of the pet shop. "Oh, Roderick, I didn't recognise you from a distance," said Sara Jane. "What a cute dog."

Cyril made it clear he didn't agree with this opinion and puffed his fur and hissed. The dog barked and ran up the nearest tree, stopping halfway up the trunk and about six feet off the ground before turning his head to bark at Cyril again. Sara Jane stared dumbfounded at the extraordinary sight of the dog seemingly caught in time while climbing the tree. "How...? I mean... Dogs can't stop halfway up a tree. Is that some trick?"

"Down, Bruno!" Roderick commanded. The dog descended confidently backwards, pausing once to note what Cyril was up to. He gave a sharp bark when he reached the ground and looked up at Roderick who turned to Sara Jane with an amused smile on his face. "Oops, that's let the cat, or rather the dog, out of the bag. It isn't a trick but it is a long story. Come around to the shop one day and I'll tell you."

"Does it have anything to do with Cyril?" Sara Jane asked, her interest piqued.

"Oh no," he replied. "Cyril is one of a kind. And, speaking of which, how are the two of you getting on?"

"Pretty well, really. But it's difficult getting him to stick to a diet. He can be very persuasive, as you know."

"Has he shown you a taste of his claws yet?"

"Nearly, but I nipped that in the bud in time. How is the shop?"

"So-so," he replied. "We're still having to deal with the aftermath of the electric eel. Fortunately, the London Zoo found space for him. So come December, he could be lighting up a Christmas tree or two."

"I read about that in the *Islington Gazette*. It all sounded very messy. I'd no idea electric eels could generate so much electricity."

"Neither did I. Jeff certainly deserves an entry in the *Guinness Book of Records*. It seems that some electric eels can adapt according to demand much in the same way as a bodybuilder lifting weights in a gym. But the trouble in the end is keeping the food supply going."

"So, is the owner suing you?"

"Fortunately, no. He realises he got his just deserts, but I don't think he'll be buying shares in green electricity any time soon. In fact, he's planning to leave the rat race altogether. Actually, I'm also about to do something a bit different."

Sara Jane looked startled. "You're not giving up the pet shop, are you?"

"Not exactly. I've been thinking about getting back into acting for some time and I've put myself down for a one-off mime performance next Friday. It's at Jacksons Lane in Highgate and I'm due on at nine, if you're interested."

"Jeez, that's brave of you. I'd certainly like to come but it depends a bit on his nibs here, if you know what I mean."

Sara Jane felt a strong tug on the lead. She glanced down at Cyril who was obviously getting bored with the conversation. "I think Cyril's trying to tell me something. We ought to get back home before the claws really do come out."

"Probably wise," replied Roderick. "I'll look out for you in the audience."

He glanced down at Bruno who was examining his paws. "Take care of yourselves," he said smiling. Before walking away, he bent down and stroked Cyril who responded with a deep purr.

Sara Jane watched the two of them walk back towards the park entrance and could have sworn Roderick's hair had turned back to blond, although it must have been a trick of the light. She also realised she'd forgotten to mention Sam, her playwright friend, who was always interested in meeting handsome, young actors.

Sara Jane and Cyril shared a large can of tuna for supper: that being diet food for Sara Jane and a treat for Cyril. Cyril clambered on Sara Jane's lap for a spell of lowest common denominator TV viewing and the two of them fell asleep, purring and snoring respectively, oblivious of the onscreen antics of the C-list celebrities. Some realisation of bedtime broke through into Sara Jane's consciousness and she gently pushed Cyril towards his luxuriously appointed chair.

Struggling to get to sleep in the Indian summer heat even with the bedclothes pushed back, Sara Jane heard persistent scratching at the bedroom door. This took her by surprise as Cyril usually kept to his part of the bargain when it came to respecting her privacy. It crossed her mind that perhaps tuna given as a treat rather than as a reward might have confused him. She turned over and tried to block out the sound of the scratching with pillows. The scratching stopped suddenly and she concluded Cyril must have given up the fight with the door. But she was wrong. His riposte started off as an itchy feeling somewhere inside her brain that wouldn't go away. It wasn't exactly unpleasant but she knew there would be more to come. Should she give in and open the door or stick it out? For chrissake, this was only a cat playing with her head just as he'd play with a toy mouse. Cyril could hardly cause her harm. But what if he regarded her as a real live mouse and she was the prey? She shivered and then, bit by inexorable bit, Cyril turned up the intensity of his incursion into her mind. Roderick had described the experience like being clawed inside one's brain and she could see he wasn't kidding.

"Get out of my fucking head, Cyril!" she shouted. Almost as suddenly, Cyril switched to the oh-so-delicious warm hug. Sara Jane heaved a sigh of relief, glad it was all over, and let her head sink back into the soft down of the pillow. Scarcely half a minute later, the scratching feeling returned and she clasped her head with both hands. "Fuck you! Stop playing with my mind!" she screamed. She crawled out of bed in search of the bedroom door, stumbling over furniture and staggering around like a drunk. She grabbed the handle and wrenched the door open, half expecting to find Cyril transformed into some bloody-fanged fiend from a horror film.

Cyril was calmly sitting on his haunches by the bedroom door. He looked up at Sara Jane, his wide-open eyes like deep, unfathomable pools. The feeling inside her head stopped abruptly. Cyril raised himself up and walked past her into the bedroom without waiting for an invitation to enter her private domain.

"Okay, you win this time, Cyril, but don't think you're making a habit of it."

Cyril stood hesitantly at the base of the bed and watched as she got under the bedclothes. He clambered on the bed and settled himself at her feet, purring victoriously and undoubtedly there for the rest of the night. Exhausted, Sara Jane relaxed into the mattress and allowed Cyril's big, warm hug to envelop her.

Cyril was back on his cushion when Sara Jane got up the following morning. She tried to convince herself the horror of the night was a dream but had to resign to the reality of what she'd gone through. So what the hell was she going to do about it? Despite being a born sceptic, she'd accepted what Roderick had said about Cyril's unusual communication skills and had bought into it hook, line and sinker. There was clearly no mileage in returning to the shop and complaining noisily that the goods weren't of merchantable quality. In these days of economic austerity, getting more than you expected was something to praise. But perhaps others had had a similar experience. She crossed to her desk and did a Google search for 'cats + unusual abilities'. *Extra sensing abilities* was second on the list of over twenty million results, but this concerned cats foreseeing danger during World War II and other times of conflict. She couldn't immediately find anything involving human beings. She entered 'cats + extrasensory perception' next and was astonished to see more than seventy thousand hits. One of these related to a cat named Oscar who seemed able to predict when New England nursing home residents were about to die by stretching out on the bed beside them. Critics pointed out that these 'extrasensory' talents represented cats using their usual senses to perceive subtle changes in the environment, including smells from bodily processes.

Sara Jane had almost given up on her trawl through cyberspace when she came across a jokey looking post in a cat forum headed 'Can't Get You Out Of My Head'. But what the poster had experienced, and what she was attributing to her cat, wasn't a laughing matter and not unlike Sara Jane's night of hell. She scanned through the replies and saw that they ranged from the vaguely helpful to the downright sarcastic, including the blunt but to the point 'see a shrink'. Her interest stirred, she sent the poster a private email although she doubted she'd receive a reply given the date of the original posting. But only five minutes later there was a reply in her inbox from someone called Alison. It was brief and didn't give much away, but it invited Sara Jane to call her on a London phone number. She dialled the number on her mobile phone.

"Alison Douglas here. To whom am I speaking?"

The voice sounded English and was unusually formal, as if she was putting on a voice or was used to screening for cold calls.

"Hello, Alison. It's Sara Jane here. We've been exchanging emails."

"Ah, Sara Jane, I'm so glad you called. I think I may be able to help you. Would you like to meet?"

Sara Jane was momentarily taken aback by her forwardness. "Well, yes, I would, but wouldn't you like to hear more about my cat first?"

"You can tell me when we meet. What are you doing right now?"

This was a woman who didn't waste time, Sara Jane decided. She briefly wondered what she might be letting herself in for but in the end curiosity got the better of her. Alison Douglas lived at the top end of the Piccadilly line, which meant a half-hour journey from the nearby tube station. She gave Cyril a glance as she left the apartment. He briefly looked up at her and then returned to his usual daytime occupation of sleeping: *perchance to dream*. But do cats dream, she wondered? Flopped on the cushion like that, it was impossible to think of him wilfully causing pain. She reminded herself that he didn't have the faintest understanding of what he was doing and was following some base instinct that had been genomically hard-wired over the millennia. But it still hurt like hell.

As Sara Jane crossed Holloway Road to the station, she reminded herself how much she dreaded having to use public transport, particularly when passengers displayed their inalienable right to a half metre of space. The scornful looks she attracted were bad enough but some of the vicious remarks about her size cut to the quick. Thankfully, on this occasion, the platform was free of men with suits, briefcases and type A personality and she could squeeze herself into a seat on the train without comment.

Alison Douglas and her cat lived on the ground floor of a down-at-heel 1950s property typical of London suburbia. The apartment was cluttered with bric-à-brac in complete contrast with Sara Jane's minimalist environment. There was also a pungent smell of urine and Sara Jane found herself inspecting the carpet for sticky, yellow patches. Alison herself was a small, rather intense, bespectacled, woman in her fifties and her precise movements and speech reminded Sara Jane of a delicate bird hovering over a flower. She wasn't surprised to find out that Alison worked part-time as a librarian. Her cat was of a similar size to Cyril and Sara Jane noticed its cat basket was under something akin to a mosquito net hanging from the ceiling. It bore a strange metallic sheen and there was a cable attached to the edge of it. Alison emerged from the kitchen carrying a perfectly laid tea tray complete with chocolate digestive biscuits.

"So tell me about your cat, Sara Jane," said Alison, pouring out the tea into bone china cups.

"Well, his name is Cyril and I'm told he's at least fifty percent Maine Coon," replied Sara Jane. "I bought him a few weeks ago. I'm not sure of his age but he's quite an old guy. He's also big which sort of suits me, if you know what I mean." She paused to sip the tea, feeling self-conscious handling the tiny cup and wishing she were holding something more robust.

"The pet shop owner warned me Cyril had an unusual way of communicating – it's as if he gets inside your head and you feel his emotions. Most of the time it's bearable, but last night, when I didn't let him into my bedroom, it was like seven shades of hell, as if my head was being scratched from inside. So, I did a search on Google for people with similar experiences, which is how I found you."

"And it's good you found me, my dear," said Alison, reaching out to place a reassuring but bony hand on Sara Jane's knee. Sara Jane found this unwanted physical contact far from reassuring and shifted her buttocks uncomfortably on the sofa. Alison continued, "You're probably wondering why a funny old thing like me would use a song by Kylie Minogue to tell the world about my problem with Bertie over there."

They both looked at the cat which remained motionless beneath the shimmering shroud. Sara Jane noticed tears brimming up in the corners of Alison's eyes. "The truth is, dear, that's what Bertie and I danced to at our wedding." For a moment, Sara Jane had a Hieronymus Bosch vision of a fat cat and canary-like human dancing under a disco glitter ball. "Unfortunately, cancer took Bertie from me a few years later and that's when this Bertie came into my life. He's not exactly a replacement, of course, but he makes me happy and talks to me."

She smiled at Sara Jane who resisted the expected response of placing a plump hand on one of Alison's knees. She was also wondering whether the visit would turn out to be a wild goose chase after all, as her host seemed a few cards short of a pack.

"I'm sorry to hear about your husband, Alison, but I'm wondering why your post in the cat forum sounded less than happy."

Alison looked nervous, as if she'd spilt the beans on something that had caused her embarrassment in the past. "Well, truth be told, my dear, Bertie and I have had our disagreements from time to time. I've learnt to be careful saying too much as doctors are apt to think it's strange, you know, like I'm a bit *loopy*."

Saying the 'L' word precipitated an impressive spasm of tics. Bertie remained where he was and indubitably wasn't about to throw any light on her sanity.

"I hope you don't mind me asking, Alison, but is that something to do with what Bertie does when he doesn't get what he wants – food, for instance?"

Alison perked up excitedly at this suggestion. "That's exactly it, my dear. You'd never believe it but he was a runt of a thing when I first got him and just look at him now..." She looked fondly at the frankly somnolent mound.

Sara Jane also looked at him; it was easy to understand who was consuming the lion's share of the food budget in the Douglas household.

"So, did you eventually manage to find a solution to your disagreements with Bertie?" asked Sara Jane, now daring to think they might share something in common even if their own nutritional states were poles apart.

"A solution?" she asked. "I suppose you might call it that, although the vet referred to it as *euthanising*."

"You don't mean...?" Sara Jane was momentarily lost for words and wondered what the hell was actually under the canopy. She sniffed cautiously and the only new smell to add was something vaguely floral that Alison was probably wearing.

"Yes, dead as a dodo – gone to the cattery in the sky, as they say. Of course, it was the last bit that cost the earth: taxidermy doesn't come cheap these days and a cat as big as Bertie needed a lot of stuffing."

"So, why the mosquito net thing? Is it a funeral shroud?"

"Oh no, dear. Bertie wouldn't stop chattering away to me even when he came back from the vet. That's when I discovered *my* solution: it's what's called a Faraday cage. I found out about it from someone on the internet. It doesn't work all the time but it helps to stop most of the radio waves that Bertie beams into my head."

"Ah, I see," said Sara Jane, wondering how she was going to extricate herself from this madwoman's parlour. "Do you mind if I use your toilet? That tea has gone straight to my bladder."

"Of course, dear, it's next to the kitchen. And while you're making yourself pretty, I'll prepare some lunch for us."

Sara Jane went into the bathroom, listening for activity in the kitchen. She noticed various boxes of pills on a shelf above the sink: a full bottle of Haldol confirmed her worst suspicions. She certainly wasn't going to stay for lunch in case some of it ended up in her food. She shivered at the image of winding up comatose under the canopy as Bertie's replacement, with some *Misery* ankle breaking next on the agenda. She eased herself out of the bathroom and crossed to the front door, opening and closing it as quietly as she could. Some workmen on scaffolding witnessed her waddling run down the street and they abruptly terminated their wolf whistles when they saw a tiny woman pursuing her, waving a frying pan. "Come back, Sara Jane! I'll make you steak and chips! We've got so much to talk about!"

Thankfully, Sara Jane was across the road and out of striking distance of the pan when Alison reached the corner near the tube station. "I'll email you," she called out to placate her pursuer.

Safely back home, Sara Jane tried to pull together something positive from the unusual sharing of Alison's preoccupations. At least a fragment of what she'd described about Bertie bore some similarity to the weeks she'd had in the company of Cyril. Euthanasia seemed an extreme solution and she rather hoped there was opportunity for compromise. It was only then she realised Cyril had broken tradition and ventured from his cushion during the daytime. "O lord, let us pray for small mercies," she said to herself in the manner of her high school teacher when waiting for her 3rd semester results. Sadly, *mercy* would never be a word that belonged in Cyril's vocabulary. He took that opportunity to squeeze himself through the dog flap, triumphantly sporting something yellow and frantically fluttering, firmly clamped between his jaws.

Coming to an abrupt stop a few inches away from her feet, he bit down with a sickening bony crunch on whatever was in his mouth. He then deposited the decapitated body of a bird with yellow plumage, followed shortly by the head itself. Blood oozed from the stump of the neck onto the kitchen floor. The bird's feet gave a final semaphoric paddle of distress. Cyril took the head back into his mouth and chewed deliberately, a few drops of blood and brain matter oozing out and staining the fur around his mouth. He looked up at her, seeking affirmation that what he'd done was good. But the smile accompanying this seemed far too knowing and Sara Jane felt a cold finger of dread walk its way slowly up her spine. *What have I done to deserve this?* Or was she overreacting to Cyril simply greeting her return home and wanting to share the spoils of the hunt? *Shit and double-shit.* She wished she'd majored in something useful like animal semiotics rather than American and English Lit. She watched as Cyril continued his gruesome feast by gobbling up the bird's body and then spitting out a few bones. She found a morbid fascination in this activity and it reminded her she hadn't had lunch and was ravenous. Once again, peanut butter and jelly exerted its magical spell and she sat down on the couch in the living room to consume the spoil of her culinary labours. Cyril jumped onto the couch to join her and rewarded her attention to his eating behaviour by giving her his big, warm hug. That plus peanut butter and jelly were a darn good combination, she decided, especially when Cyril let the warmth descend her body. She drooled and dribbled and let the day's tribulations dissipate to the accompaniment of Cyril's purring and vibrations through the couch.

At some point that evening, the reality of the day's excursion and its bloody aftermath in her kitchen sank home. Sara Jane wondered whether Alison's bizarre predicament was a portent of what was to come. The idea of a cat's emotions holding her hostage was ridiculous, but at the same time the notion of killing Cyril was equally unappealing. Overriding that was the assumption that her experiences weren't the product of a sudden descent into insanity. She'd always considered herself a logical individual and she decided to apply some of the principles of retroductive reasoning drummed into her in high school. She had two conclusions to work back from: a) that she *was* crazy; and b) that Cyril was doing something inexplicable by rational science. Her starting point as an antecedent was that she'd never shown the slightest inclination towards having an unsound mind. The strongest evidence for conclusion B had to be that others had experienced something similar or even the same, including the owner of the pet shop. But conclusion A might also be valid given that Alison had similar experiences and was probably psychotic. Or perhaps it was both A and B. Her head hurt from thinking too much.

Ordering a large pizza with her favourite toppings seemed the logical way of tackling the quandary in the short term. With her reasoning flooded by a sea of saturated fats and salt, Sara Jane succumbed to her usual vice of watching back-to-back soaps which were as good as anything at numbing the brain. She was woken from a brief doze by something rasping against her hands. She looked down and saw Cyril licking the grease remaining on her fingers. He was purring happily and rewarded her for the impromptu snack.

The dawn of a new day found Sara Jane and Cyril still fast asleep on the couch in the living room. Cyril was the first to respond to someone knocking on the front door. He pricked up his ears, yawned extravagantly and half-jumped, half-slid to the floor with a thump. The jarring sound of the doorbell followed. "What is it?" Sara Jane called out sleepily.

"Delivery!" someone shouted from outside the front door.

"Coming," she called, easing herself off the couch and excitedly awaiting the delights of another pizza.

The courier blinked in disbelief at the sight of the dishevelled woman who opened the door, hands outstretched and blinking in the early daylight like a creature of the night released from its tomb. "Are you all right, love? You don't look so great."

"I'm fine," she said unconvincingly while trying to smooth her clothes into some semblance of order. "Just give me the pizza."

"Sorry, lady, I'm not the pizza delivery. I've got your cat food here." He pointed at a massive bag of cat food by his side. "Do you want me to bring it in for you?"

Sara Jane looked disappointed. "Oh... okay, bring it in, please. Next to the chair over there will do." The courier lugged in the thirteen-kilogram bag of cat food which he placed next to Cyril's armchair. Cyril looked up at his own takeaway delivery service and emanated hungry feelings.

"I think your cat needs feeding," the courier said, puzzled at what had prompted him to say this and at the same time astonished by the size of the cat. "He's a slim one, he is," he said sarcastically, bending down to stroke Cyril's head. Cyril responded to his wit with a searing look through his green slit-eyes. He followed this with a quick scratch around in the man's head as a signal not to take that line of insult any further.

"Ow!" the courier exclaimed. "What the fuck was that!" He rubbed his head. "I'm out of here, lady. That's one weird cat." He slammed the door behind him.

Well, that was a bit more evidence to add to her retroductive reasoning. So, she probably wasn't losing her mind – at least not quite yet.

Sara Jane decided to deal with the first impediment to a more harmonious relationship with Cyril by letting him decide about mealtimes. She tilted the bag of cat food on its side and put one end in his food bowl so nuggets could fall out with assistance from his paws. She estimated that the bag would keep him going for two months even if he ate more than double his usual daily allowance. Next, she looked around in the kitchen for some aluminium foil. She'd heard of people who believed they were suffering from the effects of electromagnetic radiation constructing a hat from tinfoil to block out radio frequencies much like Alison and her shimmering Faraday cage. It didn't take her long to fashion something which looked the business and she taped it all together. She looked at herself in a mirror and decided to top it off with a beanie in case any caller might think she really had gone loopy. Cyril's gorging on his ad-lib food source reminded her how hungry she was and she cooked herself a fry-up of six rashers of bacon, three eggs easy over and four slices of fried bread. Taking her cue from Cyril, she shovelled the food into her mouth but still felt underfed. Was this her hunger or Cyril breaking through her hastily erected defence? A mound of peanut butter and jelly sandwiches finally lay the beast to rest and she retreated to the couch for a nap before lunch, with Cyril back by her side.

At some point, some subconscious drive for self-preservation cast around in her jumbled cognitive processes for another solution. She found herself dreaming about 28 Barbary Lane and considering what Anna Madrigal would do in her position. She might reach for a joint but she certainly wouldn't allow herself to turn into a plum pudding all dressed up in tinfoil ready to be steamed at Christmas. No siree, Mouse would come to the rescue and he'd exterminate the bloody cat once and for all. But she didn't have a handsome, gay *mouseketeer* in her life; okay, there were Pete and Sam but they'd be far too busy to trouble and they'd bring that horrid yapping dog that Cyril didn't get on with. Then there was Roderick, but there was something – well, *shifty* – about him. Cyril took that moment to remind her of his presence. He purred softly, she moaned quietly and let her fingers tickle her kitty.

****

Sleeping, sleeping... "Cyril, fucking don't..." Crawl out of bed for food. Cyril hungry, I'm hungry. "Christ, Cyril!" Food, food... both sated... Cyril so warm and comfortable – such a good boy. Sleep, wave upon wave of pleasure, Cyril watching, feeling his way, feeling so good… "Christ! Don't let it stop!" More sleep, more food, more Cyril...

****

Like most things planned in advance, performing at the London Mime Festival had seemed a good idea to Roderick at the time. Waiting in the wings to go on, it now appeared a very bad idea given that the mime purists in the audience were proving difficult to satisfy. Roderick had bravely chosen the Marcel Marceau classic of 'Bip as David and Goliath', but rather than dividing the stage with a screen as in the original production, he made the distinction between the characters by wearing a leotard which was black on one side and white on the other. As soon as he sidled onto the stage as the blond-haired David he realised he'd made a mistake. *Here goes nothing,* he thought. Although the performance started fine, the hecklers soon got to him and he lost control over which of his personas were meant to be playing David and Goliath. Somehow he rallied by the end and added in some bravura shimmering between the two characters as a final flourish. As he took his bows to somewhat stunned applause, with some boos thrown in for good measure, he looked to see whether Sara Jane was in the audience. She wasn't, which was probably wise all things considered.

After changing back into his clothes, Roderick sneaked back into the auditorium to watch some of the other acts. It was easy to see where he'd gone wrong: mime is mime and he'd made the cardinal sin of using what the audience regarded as trickery. He noticed people staring at him and he compounded their unease by randomly shifting between his personas. He realised he was being perverse, but having come this far, he still felt the need to elicit a definitive response. Still nothing: they obviously viewed him as an embarrassment. He sighed. Perhaps he was doomed to a life behind the shop counter, after all. He knew only too well what Brian meant when he complained of being misunderstood.

****

Pete and Sam were in their kitchen discussing checking up on Sara Jane and Cyril. "Sam, I've been thinking," said Pete, "it's been a month now since Cyril moved in with Sara Jane and we haven't seen her once. How many times is it we've phoned her?"

"It must be half-a-dozen or so," replied Sam, "and every time she's come up with some lame excuse about being busy or washing her hair or something."

"Well, I think we should phone her now and tell her we're coming by," said Pete. "We can even tell her we're bringing pizzas."

"And some treats for that bloody cat, I suppose," added Sam. He reached for his mobile phone. "Okay, I'll phone her now. You can order the pizzas."

Sam thought she wouldn't answer but eventually she picked up. "Sara Jane, it's Sam here. We're worried we haven't seen you for ages."

"Sam? Sam who?" she said, slurring her speech.

"Sam your neighbour and fellow Vancouverite," he replied with concern in his voice. "You sound rather strange, Sara Jane. Have you been drinking?"

"Oh... Sam," she said, sounding distant. "No... I've been sleeping... you know..."

"Sara Jane, we're coming by *now*. We're bringing pizzas and we're not taking no for an answer. We'll be there as soon as the pizzas have arrived." Sam disconnected the call before she could respond. He called out to Pete who'd been phoning the pizza delivery from the living room: "She doesn't sound good, Pete. Her speech was slurred as if she'd been drinking, although she said she'd been sleeping."

Pete came back into the kitchen. "The pizzas will be here in quarter of an hour. I've ordered large pepperoni times three, although that's giving her rather a mixed message."

"Anything to get a foot in the door, I think," said Sam.

After what seemed like an interminable wait, Sara Jane opened the door a crack. They couldn't prevent their jaws dropping in surprise. She was wearing a nightdress which was far from white, with food stains down much of the front. What they could see of her hair was greasy and unwashed and hung over her face like a dank curtain. A hat made out of tinfoil covered the rest of her head. She was barefoot and her feet were ingrained with dirt. She looked at the pizza boxes Pete was carrying and saliva dripped from her mouth. "You'd better come in," she said. "I wasn't expecting visitors."

Sam and Pete were shocked when they saw the state of her usually pristine apartment. Sara Jane had resorted to using the couch for a bed. It was heavily stained and surrounded by empty takeaway boxes, many of which had leaked their contents onto the carpet. The pervading smell was of stale spices, decaying food, sweat and body odour. At first glance they couldn't see Cyril, but then they saw him emerging from a large bag of cat food which had fallen over on its side. He cocked his ears and gave Sam and Pete a look of contempt, as if furious for having his eating disturbed. He'd unquestionably put on weight and it was a miracle his legs could still support his body. Cyril bared his teeth and hissed.

"It doesn't look as if Cyril's too happy we're here," said Sam. He turned to Sara Jane who'd already started eating one of the pizzas, grabbing at the slices and stuffing them into her mouth. "Christ, Sara Jane, what's happened to you? You've let things go in a big way."

"Nothing's wrong," she muttered between mouthfuls. "We're fine."

"Can we at least help you clear up?" asked Pete. He bent down to inspect a tottering tower of takeaway containers near Cyril's cushion and wished he'd brought some kitchen gloves.

Cyril hissed again and arched his back, his fur standing on end. The next thing Pete felt was an intense sensation in his head that felt like claws digging around inside his brain. He put his hands to his head. "Christ! It's that fucking cat! Make him stop it!" he shouted.

Sara Jane watched his discomfort and said nothing. She opened the second pizza box and scooped up another slice of pizza to put into her mouth. Then, bizarrely, she started massaging herself between her legs with her free hand. She moaned and a look of pleasure crossed her grossly obese face. "Please go. Thanks for the pizzas," she said, grinning broadly though pepperoni-greased lips, her left hand still rubbing away.

"Okay, we get the message," said Sam, turning to the door. "Call us if you decide you want our help."

By then, the onslaught on Pete's brain had finally abated and Cyril had returned to a position of relatively benign watchfulness. "Don't say we didn't try, Sara Jane," added Pete, joining Sam at the door. "We'll let ourselves out."

Once they'd reached the safety of the pavement, they hugged each other and the tears started flowing. "Jesus, what the hell happened there?" Sam asked, nuzzling his lover's neck. "I was frightened you were going to have a seizure or something."

"Fuck knows, love," replied Pete, touching his head to make sure it was still in one piece. "All I know is that the cat was behind it. It really did feel like it was scratching me to death from inside out."

"Did you see what she was doing with her hand?" Sam asked. "I mean, that's really gross," he added with a grimace of disgust.

"And did you see what was on her head?" Pete asked.

"Yeah, isn't that the type of thing psychotic patients wear to stop voices?" added Sam.

"And what about the state of the apartment?" Pete asked. "I hate to think what the bedroom and bathroom must be like."

"The cat appeared healthy, though," said Sam.

"Yeah, far too healthy if you ask me," said Pete. "Almost like he was masterminding the whole frigging situation."

"So, what do we do now?" Sam asked. "I mean, it's not as if she's in danger of starving herself or the cat."

"But there is that weird hat. And she's certainly disinhibited," replied Pete with a look that said 'yuck'. "Perhaps she's bipolar or something. I say we contact the local mental health guys and ask them to pay her a visit."

"Agreed," replied Pete. "I'll phone the hospital and find out who to contact. Perhaps you could speak with animal welfare and see whether they'd be prepared to get involved.

Say something about Sara Jane allowing the cat to eat itself into an early grave."

So, Sam and Pete returned to their apartment and made their respective phone calls. The local mental health unit gave Pete the contact number for a community mental health team but they told him they couldn't do anything unless Sara Jane's GP requested a visit. They recommended contacting the police if he was concerned she was at risk of harming herself. Pete and Sara Jane shared the same GP but the offhand receptionist made it clear Sara Jane would have to request her own appointment. Sam's call to animal welfare hardly went any better and the woman at the other end of the phone laughed when he said he was concerned about Cyril being fed too much.

"Well, sweetie, I think our hands are tied," said Sam in a tone of utter exasperation. "If those guys won't do anything all we can do is keep an eye on Sara Jane from a distance."

Over the next month, Pete and Sam tried to remember to phone Sara Jane at least every week. She picked up the phone on one occasion but apart from that it went unanswered. They tried to convince themselves she'd forgotten to pay the phone bill and neither felt like paying her a repeat visit after Pete's experience in the apartment. Paradoxically, Sara Jane's plight brought them closer together than ever. A week away in Ibiza, with Mr Choo in kennels, helped them to focus on life in the here and now.

****

One morning, a week or so after returning from their holiday, Mr Choo dived through the dog flap, yelping loudly, and ran manically around Pete and Sam's kitchen in danger of being trampled underfoot. "What's up with that damn pooch?" Sam asked. "He's been spooked all morning and won't touch his food."

"Perhaps it's something he's seen in the garden," replied Pete. "It could be a dead animal or something. You know what a sensitive soul he is, particularly given we've been on vacation. Try going outside with him and see where he takes you."

Sam opened the kitchen door and went into the garden with the Chihuahua. Mr Choo continued his shrill barking and headed straight towards the fence which separated their garden from that of a neighbour on the street running parallel to theirs. Mr Choo stared imploringly at Sam and then pushed his way through a gap in the fence. Sam could hear his yapping receding into the distance as he ran up the neighbour's garden. At that point, Pete joined Sam in the garden. "What's up, then?" Pete asked.

"Well, you're right about him wanting to go somewhere," Sam replied. "He headed straight for this fence and made his way into the garden."

"Christ, that's Sara Jane's garden!" said Pete looking ashen.

"Jeez, you're right," said Sam. "Perhaps she's fallen outside and can't get up – you know how big she's got recently. Give me a leg up and I'll go and find out."

With a fair amount of effort – largely because he was unfit, but also because Pete didn't want to get his clothes dirtied – Sam landed with a thud on the other side of the fence. "I'll ring you when I've got to Sara Jane's back door," Sam said. Pete heard him making his way up the garden. Mr Choo had joined him and was leading the way with his earnest barking.

Sam glanced around the garden and couldn't see anything obviously amiss. There was no sign of Sara Jane lying on the ground unable to move. He saw Mr Choo running towards the flap in the kitchen door and his barking became even more insistent. Sam's stomach roiled in expectation of what lay beyond the cat flap and he wished Pete was there with him. Gently pushing Mr Choo to one side, he stuck his head through the flap, appreciative it had been designed for a dog rather than an overfed cat. There was no light on in the kitchen but he could make out a corner of the living room through a gap left by the half-open kitchen door.

"Are you all right, Sara Jane?" he called out.

There was no reply and his nostrils registered a smell which didn't belong in Sara Jane's immaculate apartment, vaguely reminiscent of meat that had gone off but with an added, cloying sweetness. His stomach flipped again and he was certain he'd vomit. He squinted and was sure he could make out something flesh-coloured on the carpet. Suddenly, the object moved a few inches to the right as if pulled by something. He called again, "Sara Jane, make a noise if you can hear me."

The flesh-coloured object moved jerkily a few more inches. Mr Choo's bark became even more shrill and insistent. A large, white object came into vision and Sam experienced the strange feeling of the feral joy of clawing and biting food. Cyril's slit-like eyes bore into his brain and he felt something like a claw scrape his spine. The animal's canines were stained and his mouth dripped red. Sam finally succumbed to what his stomach had been trying to tell him all along and he vomited his breakfast. Mr Choo took one look at Cyril's face as it emerged from the cat flap and yelped his way back down the garden. Cat two, dog zero.

The police and paramedics arrived within a few minutes of one another following Sam's call. He'd kept the information succinct and simply said he was worried someone might be dead. Neither Sam nor Pete could face seeing what had happened to Sara Jane, so they remained outside on the pavement while the police gained access. Mr Choo had been left behind as his vocal distress was on the verge of becoming a public nuisance. A young police officer emerged from the front door, appearing shaken and ominously green, and promptly vomited into the plant pot. He looked up at Sam and Pete and shook his head before vomiting again.

"Is it that bad?" Pete asked, walking down the steps to aid the police officer.

"I'm afraid so, mate," said the police officer. "She's not a pretty sight and I don't know how we're going to get her out. The weird bit is that there's this large white cat watching us and we've all got this feeling we're hungry. But the worst thing is that the cat's been chewing bits off her." He put his hand over his mouth. "Oh shit, I'm going to be sick again."

Just at that moment, a fire engine arrived. A fire officer jumped out of the cab and breezily announced, "I gather you've got a problem with a body."

Sam was going to say something about respect for the dearly departed, but thought better of it when he noticed the massive pickaxe in the officer's hands.

"Down here, mate," called out the police officer. "She's too big to get through the doorway, so you'll need to remove the window frame."

"That's made my day," replied the fire officer sarcastically. "And I suppose you'll need our winch as well."

Removal of the window frame took no more than minutes. Getting Sara Jane's naked body into a body bag in the apartment and then onto a mega-stretcher to attach to the winch took the best part of half an hour. From the post-mortem changes the paramedics estimated she'd probably been dead for about three days. The cause of death was believed to be her heart finally giving up its struggle to support her obese body. Rather bizarrely, they noticed she had a beatific smile on her face at the time of death. She also had a number of fingertips missing. Abdominal bloating on top of her morbid obesity added to their difficulties and they were wary of her abdomen splitting open from the build-up of gases. Eventually they succeeded in getting the body out through the window and into the ambulance in a reasonably intact state.

Cyril had emerged from the apartment and sat at the top of the steps watching the proceedings. Numerous inhabitants from houses on either side of the road had joined him. He showed no outward emotional response to his owner's premature departure and no one dared bend down to stroke him once they'd noticed the blood-stained fur around his mouth. Every now and again, Cyril cast hungry feelings to the onlookers and a couple of neighbours went into their apartments and returned with bowls full of food. The police put out a request for animal welfare to attend, as Cyril definitely wouldn't be returning to the apartment.

A friendly, female RSPCA officer duly arrived and Pete and Sam gave their side of the sorry story. Another police officer came out with Cyril's cushion and feeding bowl to help him acclimatise to wherever he was heading next. The RSPCA officer's first task was to get Cyril into the van, although this proved surprisingly easy once she'd deposited his cushion on the floor of the van and added some food to the bowl.

"What will happen to him?" Pete asked, vaguely wondering whether he and Sam should offer to look after Cyril, although knowing full well neither Sam nor Mr Choo would agree to that. "He won't be put down, will he?"

"I wouldn't have thought so, love," the officer replied with a smile. "After all, he was only finding a source of food when nothing else was available. That may sound gruesome, but it's natural for cats. We need to get him checked out by a vet, though." She closed the door to the van. "Was she a friend of yours, then?"

"Sort of," replied Sam. "Like us, Sara Jane is – sorry, was – from British Columbia and our paths used to cross occasionally. We tried to help out when she became housebound after Cyril moved in, but he wasn't having any of it, so we didn't see much of her after that. Cyril was big before but he's massive now and she'd also put on a lot of weight. I suppose she was bingeing on takeaways and he was stuffing his face with cat food. I wish we could have done more but Cyril isn't a cat who takes kindly to strangers."

"How come?" asked the RSPCA officer. "He seems very friendly now."

"Just you wait," said Pete. "If he wants food or gets angry with you, he'll let you know, but not by miaowing or anything like that. Sara Jane called it being *Cyriled*: it's as if he can get inside your brain and claw you into doing what he wants."

The RSPCA officer's expression made it clear what credence she gave to this explanation. "Really? Well, let's see what the vet says about him." She opened the driver's door. "It's been good talking with you and I'm very sorry about your friend, but it's time for me to get back on the road with the cat."

Pete and Sam watched the van's departure. "I wonder what'll happen to him," said Pete.

"He'll probably take over someone else's life," replied Sam. "He's a bloody monster and I'd put him down if I were the vet."

"You don't seriously think he killed Sara Jane, do you?" Pete asked incredulously.

"Directly no, but I'd bet a thousand dollars she'd still be alive if she hadn't visited the pet shop and got taken in by the owner," replied Sam.

"So you won't be paying him a visit for old times' sake?" Pete asked mischievously. "Roderick is rather cute, after all. You know what a soft spot you have for grey eyes."

"Don't you mean green eyes?"

"No, definitely grey – plus short, dark hair – very sexy."

"I remember green eyes and long, blond hair – not quite so sexy."

"Actually, I remember him saying he used to be an actor, so perhaps he was putting on a disguise."

"Hmm, if he's that good at disguise he might be suitable for the play I've been writing. Perhaps I ought to pay the shop a visit."

"You mean the one with the murderous twins?"

"Yeah, although the difficulty is that the twins need to be on stage at the same time."

"Well, if you're going to suss him out, I'm coming with you."

****

The RSPCA van arrived at the animal hospital ten minutes after collecting Cyril. When the officer opened the back of the van she saw that Cyril had finished his food and was ostensibly asleep on the cushion. She didn't relish carrying him in or getting him into a carrier, so she cautiously attached a leash to his collar while stroking his head. He stood up slowly, shook himself, stretched a back leg and then jumped to the ground outside the hospital as if foreseeing the imminent check-up and determined to put on a good show.

The vet recognised Cyril as soon as he walked into the consulting room. "Well, well, it's young Cyril," he said. "I wondered when we'd be seeing him again." The officer and vet bent down intending to transfer him to the examination table, but he astonished them by leaping onto the surface. He looked up at the two of them like an expectant patient and was breathing rather heavily from his exertion.

"Well, I never," said the vet, reaching for his stethoscope. "It takes some strength to do that when a cat weighs as much–" He studied the digital readout on the table, "–Christ! He's more than eighteen kilograms now!"

The vet systematically went through the usual examination for an older cat. Surprisingly, given the conditions under which he was discovered, Cyril's coat was in good condition although heavily stained by blood. There was also blood around his mouth and his teeth had obviously been tearing and chewing recently. "Do we know what he's been eating?" asked the vet, half-expecting but dreading the answer. "Is it the blood from birds or mice?"

"Well, he'd obviously been eating whenever he wanted from a large bag of dry food which was on its side," replied the officer. "But when that ran out he had to look elsewhere." She looked uncomfortable with divulging much more about his recent dietary extremes.

"Oh god, you mean it's human?" exclaimed the vet.

"I'm afraid so."

"So should I take samples for forensic analysis?" he asked, looking worried and plainly not sure of the protocol for dealing with an animal that had resorted to nibbling its owner.

"I suppose so," the officer replied, "and you probably should bag the samples and use gloves to avoid contamination of the evidence." She reached for her mobile phone. "While you're doing that I'll see whether the pet shop will have him back for the time being."

The vet carefully cut away a few clumps of blood-matted fur which he gingerly dropped into some specimen bags. He then used wipes to clean the fur as best he could, although he started to feel the effect of Cyril's displeasure at this incursion into his private domain. He noticed one of Cyril's eyes had the early stages of cataract formation that was common in older cats and notably the Maine Coon. Cataract or not, he felt under close scrutiny while he was going about his business. The vet listened to Cyril's heart and lungs and thought he detected a cardiac murmur although it wasn't easy to be certain through all the fat and fur. An abdominal examination proved to be even more futile. He considered arranging an echocardiogram but decided Cyril's age didn't warrant further investigations.

The officer finished her phone call. "Yes, the pet shop will have him back although they're obviously upset to hear what happened to the owner."

She started gathering Cyril's chattels ready for his short journey back to the pet shop. Just then, Cyril started repetitively retching and expelled an object onto the examination table that was an inch long by half an inch in diameter – and it wasn't a hairball. The officer took one look at it and felt distinctly unwell. "Oh fuck, I'm going to be sick," she managed to say before reaching the sink just in time. The vet turned from writing his notes and inspected the object: a remarkably clean, distal portion of one of Sara Jane's fingers lay on the table. He grimaced, picked it up with a fresh pair of tweezers and deposited it in another specimen bag.

Cyril was dropped off at Wet & Wild by another RSPCA officer who'd taken over the duty from her colleague following Cyril's grisly, Oscar worthy performance. "He's a massive one, he is. It must cost a fortune to feed him. They tried to clean him up a bit but he wasn't having it. He seemed rather attached to the cushion, so I've brought that, too." Roderick and Cyril exchanged glances. Cyril yawned as if bored with the procedure of returning him to the pet shop. The fur around his mouth had a pinkish hue and there were a few patches where something dark red remained stuck to his fur.

"Will any further action be taken? You know, given what happened to Cyril's former owner?" asked Roderick.

"You mean, putting him down? Gosh no. It was only his survival instinct, after all. I mean, if you were starving and had a dead cat next to you, wouldn't you do what came naturally?"

Being vegetarian, Roderick wasn't convinced. "It's not the same when a person has died."

"But the principle is the same: meat is meat wherever it comes from."

He felt distinctly queasy. "I suppose so." He paused. "I take it she was dead at the time."

"Oh yes. The post-mortem put her death at least 72 hours before she was found. But the funny thing is that she had a large smile on her face, as if she'd been enjoying something."

"Oh god. Perhaps she'd been Cyriled."

"*Cyriled*? What's that?"

"Oh Cyril has this way of making people feel rather happy."

"It's funny you should say that, but I felt something similar when I was bringing him here. It was like a big, warm hug but it went a whole lot deeper." She blushed.

"That's undoubtedly being Cyriled," said Roderick. "The previous owner described it in exactly the same way. But he doesn't do that with me. He's definitely a woman's cat."

"That's creepy." She shivered. "I think I should leave before I give in and take him home with me."

The RSPCA officer left the shop after giving Cyril a final stroke. He looked at her disdainfully like a suitor who's been rejected.

"Come on, Cyril," Roderick called. "Back on your chair. We need to get you slimmed down ready for the next customer. And I don't want you using your claws on me."

Cyril climbed onto his favourite cushion, settled himself contentedly and gave Roderick a big, warm hug. He was looking forward to his next tasty morsel of pink flesh.

Chapter Four

Bruno

Bruno had been in the pet shop for a few weeks. He'd settled in well and only occasionally drove Roderick mad by climbing up the wall and then refusing to come down. More alarming still was when he chose to traverse the ceiling and come to a halt above a tank of exotic fish. Thus far, there hadn't been any accidents, but Roderick still didn't entirely trust the adhesiveness of Bruno's gecko-enhanced footpads.

As with many of the animals that found themselves housed temporarily in Wet & Wild, Bruno's provenance was shrouded in mystery. He'd arrived in an industrial looking cage that hinted at time spent in a laboratory. Someone had cut off a name tag around his neck in haste, leaving 'BR#1...' as the sole clue to his experimental alter ego, so Bruno became his name. He was also an unusual breed, a Tibetan terrier, which Roderick discovered were descended from one of the most ancient of dog breeds. Apparently these were bred and raised in monasteries by lamas over two thousand years ago and, besides doing the usual thing of herding sheep, they were also used to retrieve articles which had fallen down mountainsides.

Exactly why a shaggy Tibetan terrier should have been chosen as an experimental subject would never be known. The breed's broad, flat feet and their historical propensity for climbing steep slopes certainly made them a candidate for some genetic jiggery-pokery, but the hair did tend to get in the way. Tibetan terriers need the hair between their toes regularly trimming, especially if they're required to climb walls or suspend from ceilings. This fact might explain why Bruno found himself in a pet shop rather than engaged in some doggy derring-do for the intelligence services.

Like terriers in general, Bruno was an outgoing, friendly dog, although he was apt to be wary of clothing resembling a white coat. There was no question that he needed a home but trying to explain his unusual background would be difficult.

"Daddy, daddy, I want that dog!" demanded a rotund child who'd just entered the shop with her father. Her whining, high-pitched voice was enough to make anyone run a mile and Bruno did what came naturally to him and climbed the wall to escape the sound. Roderick noticed the reaction and thought he'd better intervene before the child cried and her father became indignant. He switched to his Rick persona to add some gravitas.

"I'm sorry about that, but Bruno gets a bit anxious when exposed to loud noises," Roderick explained, forcing himself to smile at the child. "He's actually a very friendly dog."

Father and daughter remained speechless watching Bruno who'd just reached the ceiling. Bruno went "Woof!" when he heard Roderick's voice and descended backwards to the floor.

The girl's father was the first to find his voice. "Forgive me for being blunt, but that dog just climbed the wall. That's just not possible."

"I want that dog, Daddy!" interjected the girl forcibly.

"Sweetie, you know what you have to say if you want something," reminded her father.

"PLEASE!" she added loudly.

Bruno took that opportunity to retreat to his food bowl from where he surveyed those involved in the potential transaction. Having never been available on the open market he didn't appreciate that being sold meant leaving the pet shop for pastures new. However, he did remember being in a cage and human beings wearing white clothes feeding him and hurting him with sharp objects. He found it difficult to reconcile feeling comfortable in the company of nice humans like Roderick with memories of bad people who kept him locked up and caused him pain. He wasn't at all sure what to make of these new humans, although he'd already decided the small female's shrieks were best avoided.

"So how the heck is he able to do that?" asked the girl's father.

"He's got special paws which allow him to grip smooth surfaces," explained Roderick.

"That's the first I've heard of a dog being able to do that," said the potential customer disbelievingly.

"Well, to be honest, he's a dog and a bit more," said Roderick, wondering how much he would have to disclose.

"What's the 'bit more'?" asked the man.

"Gecko footpads," replied Roderick.

"You mean as in gecko lizards?"

Roderick nodded. "It's a long story."

"I bet it is." The man looked around at his daughter who was lavishing affection on Bruno which he was happily lapping up, now she had quietened down. All of a sudden dog and child became fused together. Both tried to pull away; the child squealed and Bruno barked.

"What's your daughter's name?" Roderick asked.

"Susie," the father replied, looking concerned and then turning to glare at Roderick. "What's that wretched dog playing at?"

"Sir, I can assure you he's only playing."

Roderick called out, "Susie, be a good girl and keep still. Bruno is a special dog and gets a bit stuck now and again. I'll help him let go of you."

Roderick bent down to inspect Bruno's front paws. The child had grabbed a paw suddenly and the gecko adhesion had fixed Bruno's paw to the palm of her hand. This was similar to what happens with a gecko itself, but Bruno didn't have the same digital hyperextension as a gecko to unpeel his paw. "Well, here's another fine mess you've gotten me into," Roderick said, taking hold of Bruno's paw and gently extending the paw until it freed. He looked at the child's hand. "There, no harm done and Bruno still wants to be your friend."

Bruno wagged his tail animatedly. "Woof! Woof!" he added by way of thanks.

"Can we take Bruno home with us *please*, Daddy? I think he's really special."

"What breed is he?" asked the father who'd been watching with interest how Roderick had freed his daughter.

"A Tibetan terrier," replied Roderick. "They're one of the oldest dog breeds and you won't find many like him in the UK. As you can see, they're good with children and they're also lively and active."

The father looked at his daughter who'd resumed her bonding activity with Bruno with neither appearing perturbed by their sticky encounter. "Well, I suppose looking after an active dog could help her to lose a few pounds. Her school is always on at us about her weight. Unfortunately, her mother does indulge her something rotten."

He was also thinking about the social cachet his wife would attach to owning such an unusual dog. "How much is he?"

"He's rather expensive, I'm afraid," said Roderick, prevaricating. "Dogs with his pedigree aren't easy to come by."

"Okay, I get the message. How much?"

"A thousand pounds."

"And what if I was to make an official complaint to your landlord about the dog attacking my defenceless daughter?" he asked with a sneer.

Roderick disagreed with the 'defenceless' description but made some swift calculations nonetheless. "Eight hundred," he said, wishing this man and his Violet Elizabeth-like creature had never entered the shop. He shimmered briefly.

"Seven hundred," the man countered, not noticing Roderick's moment of emotional turmoil.

"Seven fifty," said Roderick, as a final, determined riposte.

"Agreed," the man said, pulling out his chequebook. "Is there anything else I need to know? Hydrofluoric acid for blood? Unusual dietary requirements? Oh, and is he microchipped?"

"Normal canine blood as far as I know and just standard dog food," replied Roderick. "If he does a lot of climbing you'll need to keep the hair trimmed between his toes. And he does have a microchip, although it's an enhanced one."

"What's an *enhanced* microchip," the man asked suspiciously.

"I've got a leaflet on it somewhere," Roderick replied, pulling open a drawer to search for the relevant piece of paper. "Ah, here it is. Let me see… it says here it's the latest generation with GPS and something called 'AirPower' to keep the battery charged up."

"Show me," the man demanded reaching for the leaflet. He scanned the text. "Hmm, that's interesting. It uses any WiFi signal to charge the battery and the GPS is so the owner can track their pet's movements." He was already imagining the jealous look on his friends' faces when he described acquiring a gadget they had absolutely no chance of owning. "Does it cost extra?"

"No, it comes with the dog," replied Roderick, immediately regretting he hadn't attempted to claw back some of the discount the man had coerced. "The manufacturer only made a small number of the microchips, so I suppose they're prototypes. They're meant to last the lifetime of the animal."

"So, if the dog was to get out of the house, he couldn't get lost?" asked the man.

"That's the idea, I believe," replied Roderick, "but he'd need to be in range to pick up the transmitter in the microchip."

That final comment put the man in *Gadget Show* heaven and he even paid extra for a pet door which could read Bruno's microchip. Father and daughter walked out of the pet shop with Bruno straining on a lead, feeling very pleased with themselves. Bruno was already hatching an escape plan.

****

Bruno entered the fold of the Roberts family with a flourish and a fanfare. Their house had been extensively rebuilt to include an impressive double-height dining room cum hall. Bruno's response to seeing all the bare concrete and glass was to launch himself at speed into space and within twenty seconds of his arrival he was twenty feet up the wall and about to walk across the glass canopy. But before that he farted noisily and expressively, as if wanting to imprint his presence on the prissily clean landscape. Susie giggled and her jowls wobbled. "Daddy, Bruno farted!" she exclaimed delightedly.

Susie's mother appeared from the kitchen to determine the source of the unusual sound she'd just heard while doing the prep for the evening's dinner party. She couldn't avoid noticing that Susie and her husband were craning their necks to look at something on the roof.

"What. Is. That?" she asked with a look of frank astonishment. From her vantage point and without the benefit of her designer glasses, it probably would have been difficult to establish the identity of the object currently suspended from the roof. It was also rather a comical sight given that Bruno's shaggy coat and floppy ears were dangling downwards.

"Down, boy!" ordered George, her husband. Bruno refused to budge and George was already anticipating making an angry call to the pet shop to get him unstuck.

"Come on, Bruno," called out Susie. "Walkies!"

Although there was no reason why Bruno should have responded to that exhortation when he'd never been exposed to dog training courtesy of Barbara Woodhouse, he did nonetheless move from the precarious position and padded across the glass and then down the wall.

"Well?" Diana Roberts demanded, her arms crossed with implacable intent over her chest.

"It's a dog, darling," George explained pathetically.

"I can see that it's a dog *now*, but why a dog, for chrissake? And who gave it permission to climb up the wall? You know I can't abide muck and dirt in this architectural masterpiece you insisted on building."

"Sorry, dear, I should have asked you first," George replied. "Actually, he's quite a rare breed – a Tibetan terrier – and his feet are self-cleaning."

"I wouldn't care if it was the last of its kind in the world," Diana responded huffily. "And it might as well have brushes on its feet for all I care," she added for extra effect. "I'm going back into the kitchen to prepare your wretched dinner party and I don't expect to be disturbed." With that final retort, she turned on her heels and retreated to her culinary sanctuary.

Susie started crying. "I don't like it when Mummy shouts at you, Daddy," she said bending down to stroke Bruno. Bruno looked up at her and licked her face. She giggled and went "Yuck!" Bruno licked her face some more.

"I don't like it either, Susie," her father replied, "but you know how it is these days. But at least now you've got Bruno to lick you better when you get upset."

Susie ungracefully stood up and ran to her father to wrap her hands around his legs. "Thank you, Daddy."

"Why don't you take Bruno out for a walk, Susie? I'll try and make it up with your mother if she'll allow me in the kitchen."

When it was time for the guests to start arriving, an air of relative calm had descended on the Roberts' household. This had been aided in the main by George's promise to find a new school for Susie who was always running to her mother with tales of bullying. The fact that Diana responded without fail by indulging her in the sweet delights of the freezer compartment had convinced George the tales were as tall as she was round. Curiously, Diana had said nothing about Bruno's extraordinary aerial antics, but then George was used to his wife not asking about things she didn't want to know about. She had her mind on far more important things, of course.

While Diana was dressing for dinner, George had explored further what Bruno's microchip was capable of. The pet shop owner had been absolutely correct about the microchip using the nearest WiFi signal to keep the battery charged up. The microchip also had an unusual ability to bypass any security, so no sooner had he opened the internet browser on his laptop than he found himself looking at Bruno's current location courtesy of Google maps. The microchip definitely had to be a prototype, as he'd never come across that facility before.

The sound of the doorbell announced the arrival of the first guests. George almost wished he didn't have to go through the charade of entertaining business colleagues, as finding out more about this almost alien technology was infinitely more appealing. He'd asked Susie to keep their new pet occupied, as he didn't want business discussions hijacked by any strange behaviour.

"Amazing home you've got, George," said Frank, a man who aspired to everything bigger and better much in the same way as George himself. "Is it true you designed it all yourself?"

"More or less," replied George, feeling buoyed up by the approbation so early in the proceedings. "Of course Diana had a hand in the design of the kitchen, which is more country style and not my cup of tea."

"So, she's a bit of a country girl, then?" asked Simon, the other male guest.

"Not really," replied George. "Diana likes things that are a bit twee but doesn't care for the mess that goes with country style."

Diana had chosen to make her entrance at that point and managed to switch her expression from a glare to a smile within a split-second for the benefit of George's colleagues. Even George had to admit the time spent in her boudoir had paid off. He often jibed to others that she looked and behaved like Bree Van de Kamp from *Desperate Housewives*, but her unnervingly similar neuroticism and perfectionism had certainly come to a remarkable fruition on this occasion. There weren't many women he knew who could make red hair and a crimson dress look as stunning. George basked in the sharp intakes of breath from around the room, including those from a female colleague rumoured to have a predilection for redheads.

"Darling, let me introduce Frank and Simon," said George, holding out his hand to welcome her into the testosterone-enhanced space occupied by his involuntarily leering colleagues.

"Aren't you forgetting someone, George?" asked Simone, who brushed seductively but aggressively against him as she extended a leather-gloved hand to greet the domestic goddess. She inhaled deeply as Diana tentatively shook her hand. "Ah, *femme fatale*, how daring, my dear. I'm Simone."

Diana momentarily lost her tongue while the hostess centre of her brain was attempting to reengage with her mouth. "I'm pleased to meet you, Simone. You must excuse me. I need to check on the soup. George, will you refill our guests' glasses, please."

The vision in red disappeared swiftly back into the kitchen.

"Tut-tut, Simone," remonstrated Frank, "Didn't you promise you'd be on your best behaviour?"

"That was her best behaviour," retorted Simon.

Diana emerged triumphantly from the kitchen bearing a steaming tureen of soup which wafted aromatically towards the guests. "Dinner is served," she announced, her smile firmly fixed in place.

The guests sat down, slightly uncertain how to accommodate themselves around a table set for six. "Sorry about the missing person," George said, "but Veronica had family matters to attend to, although she might get here in time for the dessert."

In the end Diana sat at the end of the table nearest to the kitchen and George and the three guests sat two abreast down the sides. Diana ladled the soup precisely and driplessly into bowls, but lingered a little too long when serving Simone. Her thoughts were split between finding her cleavage mysteriously alluring and being sorely tempted to pour the soup inside her slinky black dress. Both notions were highly disconcerting to her.

"Delicious soup, Diana," said Simon approvingly. "What's in it?"

"It's Moroccan with some special extra ingredients," replied Diana, beaming. "There are second helpings for those who can guess what they are."

"It's certainly deliciously hot and smooth," added Simone, looking at Diana from beneath her extended eyelashes and with a special emphasis on 'hot'.

There was an air of concentrated silence as the guests endeavoured to work out what the 'special extras' might be. This was a game that Diana insisted on playing at every dinner party and George knew better than to nip it in the bud. Precisely at that moment, another 'special extra' plopped loudly into the tureen.

"I think your roof is leaking, George," said Frank.

"But it isn't raining," Simon pointed out.

They all looked up. There was a shaggy dog hanging from the roof wagging what was left of its tail. Bruno clearly enjoyed the high life, as he was back where he'd started the day and he was salivating with the smell of Diana's soup. Another drop of drool descended onto the table.

"Bruno! Down boy!" screeched Susie who'd just run into the dining room in her nightdress.

Fortunately Bruno didn't stay to savour the view or the smells any longer and followed his small owner's direction by crossing the glass and descending head first to the ground. The diners had been looking on open-mouthed, and their combined gaze tracking his journey across the skyline was as exact as a radio telescope following a pulsar star.

"More soup, anyone?" asked Diana determinedly.

Still too dumbstruck to respond, the guests weren't in a strong position to stop Diana from clearing the bowls from the table.

"What the fuck was that?" asked Simone with characteristic subtlety.

"That was Bruno," Diana replied. "He's a Tibetan terrier," she added smugly.

And that effectively closed the discussion on Bruno's lighter than air performance. The guests simply assumed his breed had conquered gravity and were content to marvel at the ingenuity of natural selection or our Lord, depending on which way they were religiously inclined. George was delighted the kudos of owning a rare dog breed had hit home and was contemplating the pleasure of being served the reheated soup for tomorrow's supper, drool included.

Somehow the rest of the evening proceeded uneventfully, or at least that was the case until Veronica arrived, breathlessly, for dessert. It swiftly became apparent there was no love lost between Simone and Veronica

"George mentioned you had family problems," said Simone acidly. "I thought your family disowned you at birth."

"Darling, it's so, so much better to be born than resurrected from the grave," retorted Veronica.

"What's that on your neck?" asked Simone with alarm.

"What's what?" said Veronica, anxiously touching her neck.

"Oh, silly me. For a brief moment I could have sworn I saw a bolt poking through the skin," replied Simone.

With the guests departed and Diana back in the kitchen loading the dishwasher, George went to check on Susie. There hadn't been a squeak out of her after she'd taken charge of the errant Bruno and he was impressed she'd established control. He opened her bedroom door ajar and peered in. It wasn't difficult to make out the plump mound under the bedclothes and he noticed a smaller hump to her right which was moving. He walked in quietly to inspect the additional occupant of her bed. Susie had often taken stuffed toys to bed with her, but he was taken aback to see that Bruno was her sleeping companion. In fact, he was far from being asleep and softly whimpered when George approached his side of the bed. He gently pulled the bedclothes back.

"Dear god, what's happened to you?" he whispered. Bruno was lying on his side and his front and hind paws were attached to Susie's hands and feet. Bruno whimpered again. There was a wet patch underneath his little body. Was this just his daughter's well-intentioned attempt to prevent another social embarrassment or did she have an ulterior purpose in depriving him of his freedom?

"It's all right, Bruno, I'll free you," he said gently. Using the technique he'd seen Roderick use in the pet shop, he gently peeled Bruno's paws away from Susie's limbs. Bruno stood up on the bed, shook himself vigorously and licked George's hands gratefully. Susie remained fast asleep in the extraordinary way children can do even when there's a war waging outside.

George pointed to a rug by the side of the bed. "You sleep there, Bruno." He was amazed to see Bruno immediately jump to the floor and lie on his side, paws outstretched, trusting him implicitly as if he didn't have a care in the world. He bent down and gently felt the region of Bruno's shoulder where he understood microchips were usually implanted. He felt something considerably larger than a grain of rice but it was well hidden by the shaggy coat. "Goodnight, Bruno," he said and closed the bedroom door.

****

"Daddy, I want to train Bruno to fetch things," Susie said over the breakfast table.

"What do you want him to fetch?" asked George.

"Balls, bits of wood and things like that," Susie replied sweetly.

George was still trying to make sense of the extreme lengths she'd taken to bonding with Bruno the previous night and thought anything that got her out of the house had to be worth encouraging. Diana was thinking having no dog in the house would mean less of a feeling she was being watched the whole time.

They both said, "I think that's a good idea" at more or less the same time. Such unanimity was a rare thing for the Roberts family. So Diana agreed to take Susie to the pet shop after breakfast in order to buy some dog treats which Susie insisted were essential to train a dog properly. She also had another motive in wanting to find out more about a pet shop which had figured frequently in the local press in recent months. But when she first caught sight of the shop front from her car she almost turned around as it looked down-at-heel and generally uninviting.

However, as soon as she walked in the door of Wet & Wild with her daughter, she could see there were hidden attractions behind the hideous frontage. In fact, the tall, dark-haired man at the till was so stunningly good-looking she could well imagine making daily trips for treats. She caught his eye and was about to introduce herself when she felt Susie tugging at her skirt.

"Mummy, look at that!" instructed her daughter.

Diana followed the stubby fingers and noticed what looked like a large birdcage full of greenery. Halfway up the cage there was an exquisite animal with bright colours seemingly rippling all along the length of its body.

"What is it, Mummy?" Susie asked, and then, virtually in the same breath, demanded, "I want one for Christmas."

"Hello. It's Susie, isn't it?" said Roderick, kneeling down to her height, having switched to the other twin's persona after seeing her mother walk in. "I didn't expect to see you back so soon."

He stood up and turned to Susie's mother. "And you must be Mrs Roberts. I'm Roderick, the owner of this emporium of animal delights."

Susie's mother appeared nonplussed. "I don't understand. There was another young man here just a few seconds ago. He had dark hair, not blond."

"Oh, I'm sorry," replied Roderick. "He must have just stepped out. He was in a rush to do something or other." He looked towards the chameleon's cage. "I see you've just met Frank. He's a Jackson's chameleon, but I'm afraid he's reserved for another customer."

Judging by the glare descending on her features Susie looked as if she was about to throw a tantrum.

"But I tell you what, Susie, let's see if we can find a nice present you can give to Bruno," Roderick said quick-wittedly. "A sort of 'Hello, Bruno' present, if you like. Then you can wrap it up in pretty paper and give it to him."

With her emotional meltdown narrowly averted by Roderick's intervention, Susie offered him a hesitant nod.

"That's very kind of you, er, Roderick," said Susie's mother, recovering her composure. "In fact, we're here to buy some treats so Susie can teach Bruno to play fetch."

"I'm sure we can help with that," replied Roderick walking them towards a display of dog accessories. "How has Bruno been? Any problems with him settling in?"

"I love him and he loves me," said Susie with binding certainty.

"No, no problems whatsoever," replied Susie's mother with a steeliness suggesting the contrary, although Roderick was hardly going to push the point.

"Bruno plopped in the soup," Susie blurted out.

"Shush," said her mother sternly, raising a finger for emphasis. She turned her attention back to Roderick and smiled disarmingly. "Now, these treats. What do you recommend?"

"Okay," said Roderick back in salesman mode. "I suggest some training treats for when Susie is teaching him something new. They come in both soft and crunchy types. The soft are gobbled up quickly so they're best given as an instant reward after he's done something well. The crunchy ones take more chewing and I'd advise giving them at the end of a training session. Both can be put inside a toy which he'll enjoy chasing around the garden."

Roderick took a few packages down from the stand. "The toy is my gift, so I'll give it to Susie to wrap up for Bruno." He handed her a toy that went by the bizarre name of 'Everlasting Fire Plug'. "And I'll also give you a leaflet which explains the principles of dog training."

"What do you say to this nice man?" encouraged Susie's mother.

"Thank you," Susie replied uncertainly, having decided the squidgy red object wasn't a toy she'd enjoy playing with.

Payment made, Susie and her mother walked out of the shop. Diana looked back through the window and noticed the dark-haired man had returned just as she left. How coincidental is that? And how come he was avoiding her?

****

Over the next few weeks, routine was re-established in the household and Bruno became, to all intents and purposes, a valued member of the family. When Susie was at school, he spent most of the time quietly curled up in a corner of the kitchen while Diana went about her wifely duties. The dog flap was installed and he had no difficulty understanding its purpose or using it when nature called. Diana was mightily relieved she didn't have to descend to scooping poop. Susie took to dog training as if vocation born and was out of the house most evenings once homework had been completed. George was in techie seventh heaven unearthing the hidden secrets of the microchip implanted under Bruno's skin. As Bruno began to explore the immediate surroundings with encouragement from Susie, so a picture built up of all the locations they'd visited, right down to time-stamped co-ordinates on Google maps. But George was puzzled by Susie's choice of locations, as they didn't seem to be wide-open spaces where they could play fetch.

That discrepancy was quickly forgotten when George discovered that right-clicking on the time-stamped locations revealed a sub-menu not mentioned in the leaflet the pet shop owner had given him. Some of the functions were gobbledegook to him but one had a microphone icon by it and was like an Aladdin's cave of covert delights. He'd stumbled on this while ascertaining Bruno's favourite spots in the house. Susie's bedroom figured high in the list but the kitchen was his favoured hangout during the day. Selecting the microphone function had started audio playing from the laptop speaker. He hadn't expected that and neither had he expected to hear Diana's voice, barely audible as if she was trying to avoid being overheard.

"You know how it is. He's always checking on me. The kitchen is the only place that's my own. And now I've got that bloody dog looking at me in that fucking dopey way all the time… Yes, of course I'd like to see you again. It's just that I have to be careful… Okay, I'll wait to hear from you."

A 'mwah' noise was followed by the sound of the phone being put down.

"What are you looking at?" she shouted to someone or something in the room. George heard rapid padding sounds and then the dog flap closing as Bruno wisely escaped her wrath.

George knew better than to say anything about the conversation. Perhaps he'd misinterpreted what he'd heard.

But breakfast was quieter than usual. Susie had also taken more care with her appearance than was customary on a school day. As well as having fastened her hair with a silver grip in the shape of a butterfly, she was wearing a silver bangle on her wrist. He couldn't recollect having seen either of them before.

"That's a nice bracelet, Susie," said George. "Where did you get it from?"

"Sally gave it to me," replied Susie without a moment's pause. "She said it went with my eyes."

"That's kind of her but I thought Sally was the one who was always bullying you," said George.

"Oh no, Daddy, Sally and I are best friends," Susie said smiling beatifically.

Following breakfast George retreated to his office with a cup of coffee to mull over the exchange at the breakfast table. He was certain of two things: a) that he'd never seen the jewellery before, and b) that Sally *was* the girl Susie complained about repeatedly. He'd also been nonplussed by the stony-faced expression on his wife's face throughout the gentle inquiry. A sneaking suspicion crossed his mind. What *were* the other 'things' she'd been teaching Bruno to fetch? He waited until he heard the front door closing behind the two of them and went down to investigate further.

George went into Susie's bedroom and saw Bruno curled up on her bed. The dog looked up at him lazily and yawned. George looked around trying to imagine where Susie might keep things she didn't want others to find. He felt uneasy about searching through every drawer and was certain she'd notice any interference. Then he noticed a small locket on a chain on her dressing table and that gave him an idea. He picked up the locket and held it out to Bruno. The dog sniffed it a few times and wagged his tail. George palmed the locket and said, "Fetch!" Bruno immediately started sniffing around, initially going to the dressing table where George had found the locket and then heading to a small wardrobe. Bruno looked back at him, wagged his tail and went "Woof!"

George bent down and patted the dog. If he discovered anything in the wardrobe he'd give Bruno a treat later. He opened the door, checking first that Susie hadn't stuck a hair across the gap between the door and surround to catch the unwary. In fact he was half expecting her to come back at any minute with the excuse she'd forgotten something. He felt his pulse racing with anticipation. Looking inside the wardrobe he didn't immediately notice anything suspicious, but then he glimpsed an ornate box pushed to the back of a shelf at a level Susie could reach on tip-toe. He gently slid it out, remembering its position and orientation. Bruno became increasingly animated and his tail wagging went into overdrive. "Woof! Woof!" was added for additional confirmation.

The box was wooden, measuring about five inches by three, and felt quite heavy in his hands. He recognised it as a Japanese puzzle box given to Susie by an aunt one Christmas. He gently shook it and was rewarded by metallic clanking noises. He replaced the box exactly as he found it and closed the wardrobe door.

As he walked into the kitchen with Bruno in tow, he wondered what other secrets were left to be unearthed. He offered Bruno some treats. "Good boy, Bruno." Putting two and two together, he was now almost certain the other 'things' Susie had taught Bruno to fetch were the trinkets she was wearing together with those locked away in the puzzle box. And with the time-stamps on the Google map locations he thought he'd have no problem identifying the dates and times she'd targeted houses for her canine version of cat burglary. He had to admit her use of Bruno's climbing skill was damn ingenious. But his difficulty was knowing what to do with the information he'd acquired so furtively. He sighed. The simple fact was that he was a coward. He could design buildings to poke up impressively into the sky, but he was incapable of standing up to his wife, and now, it would appear, to his ten-year-old daughter as well. He once overheard Diana describing him as a milquetoast to one of her female confidantes. He'd had to look up the word and reading the definition had cut to the quick.

****

Sitting in his office at work, George believed he was more in command of the situation, although it was all a self-delusion. As he should have reminded himself, the difficulty of possessing a Pandora's Box is keeping a lid on the bloody thing. So, as if on a long leash, he'd found himself drawn back to the inner workings of Bruno's microchip and he'd right-clicked on a particular and rarely frequented location in the concrete and glass edifice that had become his emotional tomb.

The initial sounds George heard were reminiscent of bad pornography, with dialogue replaced by squelchy noises and the unmistakeable sound of flesh meeting flesh. He double-checked his laptop to make sure some porno pop-up hadn't diverted him to a different website. The sounds of sex were replaced by a combination of a thump, a yelp, an "Ouch!" and a "Fuck!" It didn't require forensic analysis for him to appreciate that two of the noises were made by female human beings and one by an animal. The additional fact that all of this had come from Diana's bedroom led him to a single conclusion – the damn dog had fallen on his wife and a female lover.

George drove home without the faintest idea how he was going to address Diana's practical demonstration of her infidelity. That she had been unfaithful hardly came as a surprise after hearing the audio recorded by Bruno's microchip in the kitchen. In fact, he'd come to the conclusion that her repeated trips to the pet shop for dog treats had been a pretext for assignations with the owner. But making out with a woman in their own home was something else and definitely hadn't been on his radar. There was a bitter irony in Bruno's microchip unwittingly facilitating the private investigation of his own wife.

When he opened the front door and walked into the dining room, Diana and a woman he recognised as Simone from the dinner party were sitting next to each other holding hands. Diana had deep scratches on both cheeks and Simone had a nicely developing black eye and was holding a bag of frozen peas against her face. Bruno stood up uncomfortably when he entered and was dragging a hind limb. He woofed unhappily and came over to George to have his ears rubbed. A sudden thought occurred to George and he chuckled.

"What's so funny, then?" demanded Diana angrily.

"You know, I'd always wondered whether lesbians do it doggie-style."

"You bastard!" Diana added with venom.

"Given the circumstances, shouldn't you be the one who's acting contrite?" reminded George.

"Well, you drove me to it, you shit."

"So now, not only do I have a kleptomaniac for a daughter but a wife who's a nymphomaniac."

"You know, then?"

"You mean about Susie's stealing? Oh yes. But then clearly you knew about it as well."

"So what are you going to do about it?"

"I'm not. *You* are."

"Christ, George. You're still the fucking milquetoast I always said you were."

"And you're moving out. And you can take our despicable daughter with you."

"You heartless bastard."

"I think I can live with that. In the meantime, I'm going to take Bruno to the vet to have his leg seen to. I don't want to see you here when I return. And you're paying the vet's bill."

****

The three of them didn't realise it but their conversation reached far beyond the designedly impressive enclosure of sand-blasted concrete and glass. A man in a white coat put down his earphones and reached for the phone on his desk.

"Jim here. I'm afraid we've had a bit of a situation with our subject. It seems that not enough care was taken with his grooming. The guy in the pet shop did tell them but they didn't listen. So it's back to square one, I think... Yes, I'll send out a memo to that effect."

****

MEMO
Re: BR#1579-37/FT#1

Technology broadly successful apart from a sticky moment leading to premature termination of field test. Recommend retrieval of subject and continue further evaluation.

Chapter Five

Frank

The ping of the doorbell announced someone coming in the door. That was followed by an inquisitorial "Woof!" as Bruno went to investigate. Roderick was engrossed in checking figures in the ledger in anticipation of a visit by the VAT inspector. He'd hoped to get away with a zero-rated claim from Jeff's sale but was finding it difficult to convince HM Revenue & Customs that electric eels were intended for human consumption outside the Amazon basin.

"Brian, could you see to the new customer, please?" he called out, nose buried in the dusty book.

Someone politely coughed. "It was good of you to visit Mikey in the hospital," said the newcomer.

Surprised by the interruption, Roderick looked up and recognised Markus from Sparky's party. He lent across to shake his hand. "I'm sorry not to have noticed you, Markus. My mind was on other things." He pointed at the ledger.

"Accountant?" asked Markus.

"VAT, but that's just as bad," replied Roderick ruefully.

"I thought there was no VAT on pets."

"It all depends on whether they're regarded as potential food." He mimed rabbit ears. "So watch out, Peter Rabbit."

"Not to mention Flopsy, Mopsy and Cotton-tail," added Markus. "I'm glad I'm vegetarian."

"Me too," said Roderick.

"Woof!" said Bruno, adding his opinion, although not about vegetarianism, and expecting an introduction to the handsome stranger.

Markus looked down and noticed a shaggy looking dog with one of its hind legs in plaster.

"What happened to you, then?" asked Markus looking down at the dog.

"Woof!" replied Bruno dolefully, holding up a paw.

Markus put his hand down to take Bruno's paw but was quickly stopped by Roderick.

"Sorry, Markus, but I wouldn't touch Bruno's paws. He's apt to get a little too attached to people. Stroking him is fine, though."

Markus stroked the fur on Bruno's head instead. "How did he end up with a broken leg?"

"He got carried away by the heat of the moment and lost his grip. But he's learnt his lesson. And the plaster comes off next week. So, Markus, what did you make of Mikey when you visited him?"

"He was transformed. I couldn't believe he was the same person. It was so strange seeing him with no gel in his hair and without his wide boy persona. The doctors in the hospital put it down to the shocks he got from the eel, though that seems a bit far-fetched to me."

"That's the same as I found him. I thought he'd want his money back but he seemed remarkably philosophical about the whole experience. He sent me a card when he came out saying he'd moved to Highgate Village. Have you seen him since then?"

Markus nodded. "Last week. He's renting a quaint cottage and his piano takes up most of the space. He seems happy and he's been working like mad on a book on Bach."

"JS Bach, you mean?" asked Roderick in a tone of surprise.

"The one and only," Markus replied. "He's actually been working on it for years, although he'd kept it a secret."

"I suppose it wouldn't have done his street cred much good."

"Probably not, although we'd all have appreciated seeing a softer side occasionally."

"Like he demonstrated at Sparky's party, for instance?" Roderick asked.

"Yes, playing from the Art of Fugue was a bizarre thing to do, but he's always had a weird streak about him."

"I remember him saying, 'This is for you, Sparky'. What do you think he meant by that?"

"I can't be sure, but I think it was just him reaching out to communicate."

"I can understand that, but why to an electric eel for god's sake?"

"He said something to me about them being soul mates. You know, cast adrift, directionless and all that sort of thing."

"He said the same thing to me. But I always had him down as knowing precisely where he was going. Was that a cover-up then?"

Markus nodded. "He was pretty good at doing that."

"Like describing the eel's tank as a 'babe magnet'?"

"Right. Once he decided he was straight, he overdid the macho crap. It was painful to experience, but I put up with it because of what I felt for him."

"L-e-r-v-e?"

Markus laughed. "Something along those lines."

Roderick glanced at the back of the shop. "Which reminds me. I'd like to show you the little guy who might interest you. His name is Frank."

Roderick led Markus over to where Frank's cage was situated. The domed cage was constructed from stainless steel mesh and looked as if it might contain some rare and exotic bird. It measured eighteen inches diameter at the base and rose to a height of two and a half feet. The cage was brightly illuminated from the inside and full of lush greenery. The warmth of the light and a misting on the leaves conjured up an impression of the hot and steamy tropics. Markus peered inside looking for its occupant. All of a sudden a section of the foliage shuddered. Markus blinked, thinking it must have been a trick of the light. Two small, globular eyes were peering at him and rotating like turrets independently, which reminded him rather unnervingly of his first piano teacher, who was able to watch his hands and the music score simultaneously. She was also apt to lash out with a ruler on his knuckles when his eye-to-hand coordination lapsed. The animal in the cage suddenly extended a very long tongue that confirmed the similarity with his piano teacher. A cricket disappeared into the chameleon's mouth. Markus tapped on the mesh and the eyes rotated again. The colours on the chameleon's underbelly changed from green to yellow to orange and then back to green. The chameleon turned its head to the right and Markus noticed the impressive trio of horns which gave him the appearance of a mini triceratops. The tongue was swiftly extended again and another cricket disappeared into its mouth.

"He's terrific!" said Markus, with the look of a child receiving a much-anticipated gift. "He's a chameleon, right?"

Roderick nodded. "A Jackson's chameleon, in fact. And well done for guessing the sex, it's only males that have horns. I think he's taken to you already; he doesn't usually eat in front of strangers."

"How did you come by him?"

"He was owned by a couple who decided to move to Australia. They couldn't take Frank on the plane so I bought him off them."

"Aren't chameleons difficult to look after?"

"Yes and no. They need warmth and humidity but the cage takes care of the environment. He gets ultraviolet light from the overhead bulb and there's a water mister. They're fairly easy to feed and Frank is almost vegetarian apart from enjoying the occasional cricket. He's also particularly sociable."

Markus peered inside the cage. "What's this platform halfway up the cage? It's almost like a miniature stage."

"Ah, yes," Roderick replied, with an amused smile. "I wondered when you'd notice that." He turned to a boombox next to the cage. "I'll put some music on."

Markus immediately recognised the track from an EP he'd just released. He was about to thank Roderick for the compliment when it became clear why Roderick thought Frank might interest him. As soon as the music started, the colours all over the chameleon's body had started pulsating in time with the beat. Frank nimbly leapt onto the platform with a jump and a flick of his prehensile tail. And while he didn't exactly shake his booty, Frank's movements showed a sense of rhythm previously unheard of among the species *Trioceros jacksonii*.

"That's astonishing!" exclaimed Markus. He rubbed his eyes in disbelief. "You're sure that's not some robot?"

"There's more," replied Roderick. He pressed a key on a remote control and the flat screen TV on the nearby wall exploded into life with the chameleon's multi-coloured disco dancing. The two of them watched transfixed until the track ended.

"How come the previous owners didn't exploit his talent?" asked Markus.

"Oh, they were tone deaf and never listened to music," replied Roderick. "Although the wife was always able to tell when her husband was coming home from work as Frank started changing colours when he picked up footsteps on the path to the front door. In fact, he was quite tame by the time he left them and would sit on their shoulders."

"So you didn't know about his talent until after you bought him?" asked Markus.

"No," replied Roderick. "In fact, if it hadn't been for Brian playing music when he was cleaning out cages I'd never have found out either."

"And I take it you added the camera."

"That was Brian's idea as well. He's rather keen on putting our animals on YouTube."

Markus laughed. "Oh yes, I remember the one he uploaded of a fat cat licking himself."

"That would be Cyril who bit off rather more than he could chew," Roderick added. "You might have read about it in the *Islington Gazette*."

"You don't mean the one who ended up eating his owner?" Markus asked, looking horrified.

"I'm afraid so," replied Roderick. "Our animals do seem to have a habit of popping up in the press. And now there's Frank and his talent."

"And it's quite a talent, I think." Markus paused for thought. "How do you think he'd react to being in a hot, noisy environment like a club?"

"I think he'd be okay, particularly if it was fairly humid. Chameleons respond to sound between two hundred and six hundred hertz, so he shouldn't be too bothered by loud music outside this range. The main thing to watch for is his colour change. If he's stressed or cold he'll stay a dark brown; bright colours mean he's happy."

Markus rubbed his jaw thoughtfully. "How would you feel about me hiring him for a gig I've got next Saturday? It's a fairly small club but they've got good video equipment and I could return him the following day."

Roderick smiled slyly. "That's what I was hoping you'd say. I've got a sneaking feeling Frank is destined for more than being cooped up in a pet shop for the rest of his life. And I can get Brian to upload a video clip to YouTube."

****

Frank wasn't exactly catapulted into stardom, but the impressionable public certainly knew they were onto something good as soon as they came across the video clip. Within twenty-four hours, the video of him dancing to DJ Mista Mixa's track had attracted over one hundred thousand views and social networking sites were abuzz with enquiries about the new pop sensation. When Roderick arrived outside the gig's venue the following Saturday, he couldn't believe the size of the queue waiting to get into the club for the set. In fact, Markus's position in the evening's running order had been elevated to the prime spot and a still of Frank from the video and the tagline 'feat. Freakin' Frank' had been added to the poster.

The club was packed and Roderick was relieved his pass gave him access to an area reserved for the press. He'd gone backstage earlier to check on Frank and he'd seemed active and healthy. As the week had gone by, he'd been questioning his motives for allowing Frank to be exploited but had reasoned he wasn't being coerced into performing and could remain in a corner of the cage if he chose.

A screen went up at the front of the club to reveal Markus standing behind a laptop, keyboard and controller. Next to him, Frank's cage stood majestically, the internal lights shining mysteriously through foliage and the mesh of the cage onto the walls of the club. Markus faded up watery and hissing sounds picked up by microphones in the cage and added reverb and flanging to create an otherworldly space where even a pin couldn't drop without becoming ripples of sound. Excited whispering from the crowd turned into a susurrated mantra of "Frankie, Frankie". Markus picked up on the beat and added a crisp bass drum and softly sizzling hi hats. Multiple video projectors sprang into action around the space. As if on cue, Frank languorously climbed onto the platform and rippled his colours from the tips of his horns to the spiral of his tail. His tongue flicked out and a solitary cricket left over from his last meal disappeared from sight. One of Roderick's neighbours exclaimed, "Way to go, dude!" Markus dropped in the track used in the YouTube video and the crowd roared their approval. Frank matched the beat, rippling colours and shaking in sync, with the video feed kaleidoscopically shifting the mesmerising image around the walls of the club.

Despite Roderick's doubts, Frank gave the impression of enjoying the experience. He also had remarkable stamina and kept his colour changing and dancing going for the full hour of Markus's set. The deafening applause left no doubt that DJ Mista Mixa feat. Freakin' Frank had gone down a storm with the crowd. Roderick left the club with a ringing in his ears but he was also intrigued to see what happened next.

By lunchtime on the following Monday, Markus's agent had been bombarded with requests for sets from DJ Mista Mixa feat. Freakin' Frank. He asked Markus to drop by his Soho office for a liquid lunch to plan their strategy for unleashing his talent on the world.

"This is fucking brilliant, Marky!" exclaimed his unusually jovial agent who'd just lit his sixth cigar of the day. "I mean, you're a great DJ, but this is taking things to the next level and beyond."

Markus was about to remind his agent that Frank was just a chameleon when one of the many mobile phones on his desk started vibrating away like some hyperactive sex toy.

"Yes, who is it?" he demanded curtly. "Pete, my old buddy. Long time, no see. What can I do for you this early in the day?" He listened and the cigar almost dropped out of his mouth. "Le Grand Macabre? This Friday? 10k?" He made an A-Okay sign for Markus's benefit with his thumb and forefinger. "That's brilliant, mate. You've got it. They'll be there on Friday."

Markus wondered what he'd just been signed up to without his informed consent.

"You've made the big time, Marky mate," said his agent, lighting up another cigar. "That was Piotr Thom and he wants you and Freakin' Frank as his special guests at Le Grand Macabre this Friday."

"Le Grand Macabre as in Le Grand Macabre, Ibiza?" Markus asked, not believing what he'd just heard and wishing his agent wouldn't mess around with his name.

"Would I joke with you, son?" asked his agent both rhetorically and condescendingly. "And the best bit is you get to fly there and back in a private jet. It's from London Luton, mind you."

"Christ! I don't know what to say," said Markus looking shell-shocked.

"Don't take the good Lord's name in vain. You're doing it and you'll do it like the pro you are," insisted his agent.

Markus still looked doubtful. "What about Frank? Surely he'll need special provisions like a passport."

"No problemo. That's the beauty of a private jet. Frank goes in his little cage in the cabin. He can even have some bubbly if he wants it. I'll check about passports but I think they're just for dogs, cats and ferrets. I'll arrange a cab to collect you at six."

"What about the set?"

"Pete suggests two one hour sets. The first will be poolside in the afternoon, so have a word with your guy in the pet shop about letting Frank out of his cage. The second is scheduled for the evening with elite invitees only, so you can go to town with atmospherics and ambient crap. What sort of food will he need?"

"Well, I've been feeding him a few live crickets, plus sweet potato, carrots and spring greens."

"Okay, I'll let the hotel know. And I'll get onto a T-shirt manufacturer to get some chameleon merchandise together ready for the gig."

His agent led the stunned Markus to the office door and gave him a manly thump on his back. "And for chrissake, Marky, take good care of the fucking animal. I don't want a hefty bill from the pet shop if anything goes wrong."

Markus took a cab to Wet & Wild hoping he'd find Roderick in the shop. He found Roderick deep in conversation with his agent on the phone and Brian bouncing with unbridled enthusiasm now he'd discovered Frank was destined for party time in Ibiza. Brian also had an encyclopaedic knowledge of the Ibiza music scene and every gig Piotr Thom had done over the last fifteen years. Markus didn't share that knowledge and felt distinctly inferior and less than a pro by the time Roderick finally finished the call.

"That's brilliant news, Markus," Roderick said, looking almost as excited as his assistant. "I'm really pleased for you."

Markus *was* feeling pleased but he was thinking the act might be better described as 'Freakin' Frank feat. DJ Mista Mixa'.

"Thanks, Roderick, but I'm starting to wonder whether either of us is ready for the big time."

"Piotr Thom didn't have cold feet when he started his club night at Sacha in 2002," said Brian helpfully.

"Thanks for pointing that out, Brian," said Roderick, "but Mr Thom never included animals as part of his act." He turned back to Markus. "So what do we need to do to get the show on the road?"

"Piotr Thom wouldn't say 'get the show on the road' either. I mean, that's so OLD," interjected Brian, who slouched off back to his feeding duties.

Roderick glared at him. "Sorry, he's being an idiot," he said to Markus.

"No, he's got a point," said Markus looking more positive. "So what if I'm being hired because of the chameleon. It's up to me to prove I deserve the break."

"Yeah, man, go for it!" said Brian from the other end of the shop, giving Markus the thumbs up.

"And there's a thousand in it for the shop as well," said Roderick.

"Is that what my agent told you?" asked Markus.

"Well, he started with five hundred but I haggled for more," replied Roderick looking pleased with himself.

"He told me he'd be offering you two thousand and a rolling contract for more performances," clarified Markus.

"The bastard!" exclaimed Roderick.

"Never trust someone who has cigars for breakfast, lunch and dinner, young shape-shifter," said Markus, putting a hand on Roderick's shoulder.

"How did you know?" asked Roderick in astonishment.

"You mean about the shape-shifting?" asked Markus. Roderick nodded. "Oh, it was something Mikey mentioned. He's very perceptive. He mentioned you shimmering when he got up close." He examined Roderick's face closely. "And you're doing it now."

"Oh Christ!" said Roderick, now shimmering with a tinge of red.

"Don't apologise. It's sweet. If I take you out for a meal some time, will you tell me more about it?"

"Okay," replied Roderick coyly and keen to change the subject. "Now, what do we need to do for your flying visit to Ibiza?"

"How's Frank been since I returned him yesterday?" asked Markus.

"Fine," replied Roderick, "or at least, not obviously worse for the wear. But putting him on a plane and then in front of a noisy crowd could be asking for trouble. You'll need to keep on guard for signs of him being stressed."

"Like being more lethargic than usual and staying dark?"

"Plus being off his food and not drinking enough," added Roderick.

Markus nodded. "One of the sets I've been asked to do involves performing in the afternoon by the pool. Do you think that'll work?"

"You mean having Frank out in the open?"

"That's the plan. He'll probably be on a platform next to the laptop. Is there a risk he might run off?"

Roderick laughed. "I don't think there's much chance of him moving anywhere quickly. If it's hot and sunny, he should enjoy being outside the cage, but there's no guarantee he'll want to perform. There's also the issue of getting him in and out of the cage. Chameleons don't like being handled, so he'll need to get used to you. I suggest trying that while he's in the shop." He called out to Brian, "Would you mind helping us here, Brian. You're much better with Frank than I am."

"And what if he won't come out of his cage for me?" asked Markus.

"Well, I can come on the plane as your official assistant and chameleon handler," said Brian excitedly, looking at Roderick for confirmation.

"I think you've got a new boyfriend, Markus," said Roderick, getting back at Brian for his past jibes.

"No, I'm not," muttered Brian. "I'm just trying to be helpful, that's all."

"Roderick knows you are, and so do I," said Markus placatingly. "And I'd really like to see your magic touch with Frank."

Brian went over to the fridge on the bench and extracted a live cricket from an aerated cardboard box which he held between his thumb and middle finger. He undid the catch to open Frank's cage and put his left hand on the floor of the cage with the palm up. He waggled the cricket on his palm so Frank could see it was alive. Frank unfurled his tail from a branch and lowered himself to the floor, one eye fixing on the food and the other glancing in every other conceivable direction. Brian slowly withdrew his hand and the wriggling cricket until it was just outside the cage. Frank's roving eyes were now firmly riveted on the struggling insect. Brian moved the cricket so that it was above his wrist. Slowly but surely, Frank moved onto Brian's hand and then flicked out his tongue to swallow his reward. "There, it's easy," said Brian, looking pleased with himself. "You have a go. Get a cricket from the box and do the same as I did. He should walk onto your hand if he likes you."

Markus wasn't so certain about his animal attraction and didn't relish picking up a live cricket. He approached the box in the fridge trying to remind himself this wasn't a trial in a reality TV show. His attempts at picking up a cricket were faltering even though the insects were slowed down by the cold. Eventually one succumbed to his pincer grip and Markus returned to put Brian's confidence in him to the test. Markus could see Frank's eyes spinning overtime as he approached with his bounty. With the extended build-up, it wasn't surprising Frank barely paused for a breath before crawling onto Markus's hand and consuming the cricket.

"See, I told you so," said Brian. "He thinks you're okay."

"Let's see how he reacts to music when he's out of the cage," said Roderick, leaning across to start the boombox. Markus's track started playing but Frank just stood on his hand, his colours as vibrant as ever but not changing with the beat. Frank's eyes continued to rove, almost as if trying to lock onto a reason for being coerced from the safety of his cage.

"Roderick, try changing the EQ setting on the boombox," suggested Markus. "He's only picking up sound through the air, so you might need to add a boost at around two hundred hertz."

Roderick tweaked the EQ slider a few notches higher. Although to his ears the difference was slight, Frank's response was dramatic. Green turned to yellow, yellow to orange and orange to red, up and down the length of his body in sync with the full-on trance bass. As the track developed in complexity, so the waves of colour started to ripple vertically and Frank added a sort of wobbling dance movement. Markus was watching the chameleon with wide-eyed, dumbstruck amazement and hardly daring to move a finger lest his performance was disturbed.

"Well, that's definitely a success," said Roderick, "and Frank doesn't seem at all fazed by having to perform outside his cage."

"I've seen how he responds to my tracks, but what about mixes from other DJs or mainstream pop?" Markus asked.

Brian put up his hand. "I can't remember how I chose your EP, but I know he didn't like the CDs I found on top of the boombox." He picked up a small pile of CDs and looked through them. "Abba, Pet Shop Boys, Wham, Madonna, Kylie Minogue... they must be from my boss's pink period."

Roderick glared with a crimson hue. Markus looked at him and laughed. "Well, we share the same taste as they're all in my collection as well."

Roderick mouthed, "Thanks."

"Let's get him back in the cage," Brian said. "Markus, if you move your hand into the cage Frank should hop off."

And Frank did indeed hop off Markus's hand and then used his tail to somersault onto the platform where he continued to ripple and wobble to the music.

"Amazing," said Roderick in wonderment. "He's certainly a real trooper. Look, Markus, I suggest you take him home so he can get used to you before your flight on Friday. We can give you a box of locusts but remember to keep them in the fridge or else they'll escape and fly all over the place."

"That sounds good," Markus agreed, "but I might need to ring you if I run into problems. I was going to use the rest of the week to prepare for the gig anyway, so it'd be good to try him out with different tracks."

"Here's my mobile number," said Roderick, handing Markus a slip of paper. "In any case, call me when you know you'll be returning so I can settle Frank back in the shop. Remember to keep the water reservoir topped up and keep an eye on the temperature. Up to thirty-two degrees Centigrade in the daytime is fine."

Markus left in a cab with Frank's cage and a supply of food. "You like him, don't you?" said Brian.

"Yes," replied Roderick simply.

"So do I. He's cool," added Brian surprisingly.

****

Markus did his best to sneak Frank into his flat as surreptitiously as possible in order to avoid questions from neighbours or an interrogation from his landlord. It reminded him of the first time he smuggled Michael into his digs when he was at the Royal Academy of Music. The joyous innocence of their first kiss on the piano bench was turned into acute embarrassment when a fellow student walked in on them unannounced, and soon after that Michael became Mikey.

Markus carefully placed the cage on top of the baby grand piano. The crickets had woken up during the cab journey and he found room for them in the fridge. A plague of crickets in his flat wasn't exactly what he had in mind. In fact, another sort of black cloud had descended upon him during the cab journey as he was still struggling to see himself worthy of the prestigious gig. He idly played an eight-to-the-bar bass line on the piano, contemplating his agent's overgenerous view of his talent. The reality was he was just a minor league DJ with a dancing chameleon as the only possible claim to fame. Just thinking that made it seem ridiculous and he was about to reach for his phone to call the whole thing off. He looked into the cage and saw that the chameleon had climbed onto his platform and his colour changing was rippling away as animatedly as ever. Frank was clearly enjoying the boogie-woogie. Markus sat down at the piano and added some rising dominant seventh chords on top of the bass line. Frank rocked on his little feet to the beat. Markus stopped playing and opened the cage door. He held out his hand and Frank climbed onto it, his colours reverting to brilliant shades of green. Markus withdrew his hand and gently put Frank down on top of the piano. He sat down again and resumed what he'd been playing before but adding syncopation and key changes. Frank was in his element and his eyes were mesmerically rotating as if in a trance. After a few minutes, Markus returned Frank to the cage and fed him a few cooled down crickets. He extracted his mobile phone from his jeans and made a call.

"Jim Jam Management," announced the voice gruffly.

"Hi, Walter, it's Markus. I need a favour. Can you get me a grand piano for the Ibiza gig on Friday?"

"What's it for?"

"Something extra for the act. A new USP. You'll like it."

"I'd better." Markus heard a puff on a cigar. "A Steinway, you mean?"

"The bigger and blacker the better."

"I'll get onto it. But for chrissake, don't screw it up with some new age rubbish."

That new USP turned out to be Markus's turning point. DJing had been an easy way out of the classical music rat race and his innate talent had given him the edge on other newcomers to the scene. He'd toyed with introducing classical music into his sets before, but he'd been wary of alienating the traditionalist crowd who expected trance to stay trance rather than straying into unproven territory.

So, over the next few days, Markus put together half-a-dozen tracks incorporating boogie-woogie bass lines and bluesy chord progressions in an Ibiza techno framework and tried them out on Frank perched on top of the piano. He also discovered that chameleons appreciated slow movements and sampled Frank's hissy warnings to use in the sets. Come Friday, both were as prepared as they could be for Le Grand Macabre and it was with a real sense of excitement and only a little trepidation that Markus got into the cab to go to Luton airport.

As soon as Markus arrived at the private terminal, porters appeared to put his flight cases into the hold of the Cessna Citation parked just yards away. Security and passport control took just minutes and Frank's cage was put through a full-body scanner to check that nothing was hidden under the foliage. As Markus carried the cage and his holdall up the steps of the plane, Piotr Thom appeared in the doorway smiling.

"Great to see you, man. I'm pleased you could make the gig at short notice. I'll give you a hand with your bag."

Piotr led Markus into the plane and he was astounded to see they were the only passengers. Markus strapped Frank's cage into one of the seats and connected the power lead to a socket. Piotr bent down to peer inside the cage. "Wow, he's such a cute little thing. I love his horns. And he's so green." The captain appeared at the doorway to the flight deck.

"Welcome on board, chaps. Please help yourself to drinks and breakfast. We're just about ready to go." He joined Piotr to inspect the unusual passenger.

"So, this is our VIP. What does he eat?"

"Crickets and vegetables mainly," replied Markus.

"And I gather he dances to music," said the captain.

"It's more that he changes colour to the beat. He wobbles on his feet but it's not exactly dancing," explained Markus.

"You should see it. It's quite something," added Piotr.

"Well, I'll try to get to the gig," said the captain standing up. "And I'll do my best to avoid turbulence. The weather report is good all the way to the Balearics, so we should be okay. If you'll excuse me, I'll just go and secure the door."

Markus leant back in his seat trying to take in the new flying experience.

"Sorry about the crappy plane," said Piotr. "It's usually a Gulfstream with a couple of flight attendants, but what with cutbacks and so on, everyone's doing it on the cheap these days." He reached for a bottle of champagne and poured a couple of glasses for Markus and himself.

Markus laughed. "It seems like luxury to me. I've never been in anything other than economy."

"Well, welcome to the high life, mate," said Piotr, chinking glasses. "Here's to a great gig."

The plane started its roll down the runway.

"So, Markus, how did you get into DJing?" asked Piotr.

Markus took a sip of champagne. "Actually, I started out training to be a concert pianist."

"You mean at a music school?" Piotr asked, looking astonished.

"Yeah, the Royal Academy of Music, in fact," replied Markus. "But there were so many who were better than me, including my best friend, so I looked elsewhere for a job. I'd done a bit of DJing in my teens, so that was the obvious choice."

"And you're obviously good at it, or else you wouldn't be on this plane," said Piotr with an encouraging smile.

"I think I'm okay but I've been looking for a new direction."

"You mean Freakin' Frank?"

"Sort of, but he's more a means to an end. It was working with him that gave me an idea."

Piotr smiled again. "I think I know what it is. The grand piano?"

"You've got it. I'm pretty good at boogie-woogie and I've been working on updating that into trance."

"I'm intrigued. There are so many sub-genres there's always room for something new. I can't wait to hear your set. More champagne?"

The flight proceeded uneventfully. Markus fed Frank his breakfast and checked he wasn't getting too stressed by the new experience of flying. He was as green as ever and drinking well. During take-off, Frank had hidden away in the coolest area at the back of the cage, but once airborne he'd climbed onto the platform to get a better view of his surroundings. He'd even started displaying some ripples of colour, but that was probably because of vibrations from the engines.

Markus awoke as the plane touched down. He'd had a bizarre dream where he and Frank had swapped sizes and places, with a Frank of dinosaur dimensions playing the piano, a tiny version of himself dancing on the piano wearing a thong, and then Frank lassoing him into his mouth with his sticky tongue as an encore. He looked at the cage buckled into the seat next to him and saw that Frank was in his usual spot when he wanted to be out of the public eye. He hadn't changed in size.

The well-oiled VIP machinery engaged impressively as soon as they disembarked. Within what seemed like only seconds, they were in a luxurious people carrier taking them to the beach-side venue hosting Le Grand Macabre.

"Impressive," said Markus. "I think I could get used to this."

Piotr nodded. "Well, it's essential if you're hopping around from one gig to another."

"Where's your equipment?"

"It's gone ahead of me. There's too much to go on the Cessna and I'm here for a season anyway."

"Do you have any tips for a newbie like me?"

"I don't think you need any, mate. You've got a USP, you've got a decent agent and you've got charisma. But you can ask me again after your gig, if you like."

With just a few hours to go before his set started, Markus's immediate priorities were the welfare of Frank and setting up his equipment. As he went through the extravagantly spacious reception area up to his suite, he caught a brief sight of the pool and noticed the gleamingly black grand piano already in place. Up in his room, an array of refreshments for both him and Frank had been set out on a table. In Frank's case, this included crickets plus mealworms, sweet potato, kale and lettuce. A note had been left with contact details of a vet specialising in exotic pets. Frank's cage was already in the room and he plugged in the power cable. He reached for his phone and dialled Roderick's mobile number.

"Wet & Wild. Can I help you?"

"Hi, Roderick. It's Markus. We've just arrived at the hotel and I thought it'd be helpful if you were on the phone when I check on Frank."

"Good idea, Markus. It's pretty quiet in the shop at the moment, so I'm all yours. How did he cope with the flight?"

"Okay, as far as I can tell. He's been bright green all the time and even hopped onto the platform at one point. I think he was confusing the engine noise with a groove."

"You've got the cage plugged in?"

"Yes, both lights are working and the misting and drip have been fine all along. I filled up the tank during the flight. The temperature has been stable as well."

"Sounds good. Do you want to try feeding him something?"

"Okay. The hotel has put out quite a buffet for him. I'll try him with one of these mealworm things... Yuck, it's wriggling... Okay, I've got it now and I'm opening the cage door... Well, he certainly liked that, it disappeared down his mouth as soon as I put it on the floor."

"And he's still green?"

"Yes, as green as grass."

"What about his skin and eyes? Are they sunken at all?"

Markus inspected Frank closely and Frank reciprocated the attention. "No, he looks quite plump along his body, and his eyes are like little rotating balls."

"Fantastic. It sounds as if he's all set for his performance, but just give him a bit of peace and quiet until then."

"Thanks, Roderick. I appreciate the help. I'll give you a ring once we're on our way back."

"I'll look forward to that. And break a leg, darling," Roderick said in a plummy, actorish voice.

Markus laughed. "I'll try to."

Markus went down to the pool area to inspect where he'd be performing and to set up his equipment. It was a large space with an area for dancing in the centre plus several pools and a surrounding deck. The DJ equipment was set up opposite the central area and there were flat screens for the video feed. The grand piano was to the left of the equipment desk and he'd be able to reach across from the keyboard to trigger clips from the controller. He'd anticipated something like a Yamaha and didn't expect to see a Bösendorfer Imperial with the trademark extra keys in the bass. He set up his laptop and controller and then sat down at the piano and started playing a bass riff.

"Wow, that's quite a sound," exclaimed Piotr who'd just joined him by the piano. "Who needs synths or a PA system when you've got a monster piano?"

"True," agreed Markus, "but these black beauties cost over a hundred and thirty k back home."

"Fuck!" exclaimed Piotr. "That's serious money! So how are you planning to use it in your set?"

"I'll show you," Markus said, leaning across to start a sequence and arming some clips. There was a soft hissing sound which quickly increased in intensity and bounced between the speakers. Out of this raw sound, Markus extracted a throbbing drone designed to get Frank going. Bouncy, granular drips descended into the bass. Markus added percussive bass notes from the piano, initially random but quickly identifiable as an upbeat rhythm. An accelerating snare roll led on to the first section of the track with full on drums, bass and Markus's development of a boogie-woogie riff. He topped off the section with some glisteningly hypnotic arpeggios in the right hand and was about to drop the track back to the drone. Piotr noticed the growing crowd of hotel guests listening to the impromptu performance and leant across to lower the master faders on the mixing desk. The onlookers erupted with applause and whoops of approval.

"Sorry, I was getting carried away," said Markus apologetically.

"Don't apologise. That's fantastic," said Piotr encouragingly, "but you'd better not give away too much too soon."

By the time Markus's set was due to start there was a tangible air of expectation around the pool. Word had spread far and wide since his first gig with Frank back in London and the hotel was finding it difficult to enforce their guests-only policy. Markus started the set in exactly the same way as in London, mainly because he hoped Frank would be comfortable with something he vaguely remembered from before. This meant Frank remained in the cage with the camera over the platform feeding the flat screens. From what he'd seen so far, Frank showed no diminishment in his activity. He'd rehearsed taking him out of the cage and putting him on the platform, but he had no way of knowing whether Frank would co-operate during the live performance. In fact, within ten seconds of opening the cage door and transferring him to the platform, Frank was almost swaggering. The crowd were ecstatic and chanting, "Frankie! Frankie!"

For the last third of his set, Markus had decided to sit down at the piano and to have Frank on the lid. This was risky as there was a chance Frank might lose interest and wander off in his typically laconic way or, worse, have a hissy fit and merge with the colour of the piano. But once again, Frank surpassed himself. And so did Markus. At one point, after executing a run of sixteenth note octaves even Rachmaninov would have been proud of, he thought he caught sight of Liberace's ghost leering at him from the end of the keyboard.

The set ended with a pianistic helter-skelter into the outro and then just the panned hiss and drone for the final fade. Riotous applause erupted from the crowd. An exhilarated Markus bowed, keeping a wary eye on Frank who always seemed a little nonplussed when there was nothing to excite him. Markus put out his hand and Frank ambled onto it and then up onto his shoulder. He surveyed the noisy crowd and glowed orange with pride.

"Brilliant, mate!" Piotr exclaimed excitedly. "You've fucking made it! I think you've just put all of us out of a job!"

****

The noisily ringing phone woke Markus abruptly. He reached to answer it and groaned when he saw the name 'Walter' on the display.

"Good morning, Marky," his agent said breezily and without the usual rasp from smoking the first cigar of the day.

"Morning, Walter. You know I only got back two hours ago?"

"Sorry, mate, it couldn't wait. You've hit the big time. We've just had a request from some German prince for you and Frank to play at his birthday party. It's at the Chameleon Club in Dubai this Friday. He saw your gig last week. He sees himself as a bit of an expert on chameleons. And I hear he's on the lookout for a husband, so you could be onto a good thing if you play your cards right. Oh, and he's sending a Gulfstream to collect you. I'll email you the details." All this had been delivered in a gush to the accompaniment of mobile phones vibrating on his desktop. "I must go. Speak to you later."

****

Boarding the Gulfstream G650 at London Heathrow transported Markus and Frank to a level of indulgence neither had experienced before. A reptile expert was on board and took over the care and attention of Frank, leaving Markus to the fawning attention of two handsome air stewards who'd have done anything to satisfy their passenger. During the flight Markus learnt that his host was a wealthy, German aristocrat and also that he was only twenty-five and demanding of his employees. Somehow, Markus managed to avoid most of the excesses on offer on board and concentrated on how he'd adapt his performance to the more intimate surroundings of the evening's venue. Once they'd landed, an efficient limousine service deposited him, Frank's cage and his flight cases outside the venue.

The Chameleon Club was as blingy as everything else in Dubai. Its main claim to fame was the neon lights covering every surface, which were presumably meant to mimic a chameleon in a state of terminal excitement. A hideous model of a giant chameleon with an outstretched tongue hung ominously over the bar. His agent's email had furnished him with the bare bones of the evening's assignment but thus far he hadn't met anyone other than the technicians charged with setting up his equipment. And what should have been a concert grand piano turned out to be a Yamaha piano and an electric one to boot.

Markus's pared-down set eschewed the ambient and atmospheric additions which had gone down so well at Le Grand Macabre. He'd reasoned that a smaller, brighter space needed strongly rhythmic tracks with minimal melodic invention and a stripped-down, Detroit-type drive. The set had commenced with Frank already on top of the piano, anxiously surveying the crowd and reminiscent of a go-go dancer waiting his turn in a discotheque.

Disappointed with the reaction he was receiving from the seated crowd, Markus mixed and matched culturally appropriate references from far and wide, including Kraftwerk and Beethoven. Response from the seated crowd was muted and Markus was left wondering whether the two of them would need to find somewhere rather less glitzy to spend the rest of the night. As Markus started packing up his equipment, he saw a tall, elegantly handsome man approaching the piano.

"Congratulations, that was magnificent, Herr DJ. Count Gustav von Styffertitz at your service," announced the figure in a deep, Germanic accent and bowing at the waist. He stood up straight and smiled. "Actually, you can cut the crap and call me Gus," he added in a normal voice. "Your set was quite fabulous. We particularly enjoyed your musical quotation from Herr Beethoven even though it was rather cheeky. And I must apologise for the lack of attention. My guests were rather busy eating and drinking."

"Markus Henriksen," said Markus, extending a sweaty hand to shake Gustav's cool and precisely manicured hand, "and thanks for the compliment, Herr Birthday Boy. But I have to ask you, is Styffertitz really your name?" He was attempting badly to stifle a giggle.

"Indeed it is," Gustav replied, looking dramatically affronted, "and the 'y' is pronounced as in 'eye' for your information. In fact, I'm a descendant of a delightfully decadent Hollywood actor who specialised in bad horror movies. Sadly, he changed his name to the rather boring 'Seyffertitz' and I've never forgiven him for that."

Gustav bent down to look at Frank who was also recovering from the exertion of the set. "An excellent specimen. A Jackson's chameleon, or *Trioceros jacksonii* to be precise. Certainly mature. Do you know his age?"

"I'm not sure. The pet shop bought him from a couple who left the UK, so he must be getting on a bit. I probably should put him back in his cage."

"I'll help you. But first a little treat after that virtuoso performance." Gustav extracted a pill box with mother of pearl inlay from his jacket pocket. He flipped the lid open and took out a plump mealworm which he placed about a foot away from Frank on the piano lid. Within a fraction of a second the momentarily wriggling insect had disappeared from sight.

"I always come prepared," Gustav said to the astonished Markus, "although sometimes it's the wrong pill box. I don't think your charming chameleon would have liked to chew on strawberry-flavoured latex." He giggled. "He can have another one after we've put him to bed."

The two of them managed to manoeuvre Frank back into his cage without any major difficulties. Markus was trying to establish the identity of Gustav's citrusy, musky scent. Gustav offered Frank another mealworm from his box of tricks that was consumed just as quickly. Markus felt Gustav scrutinising him intensely as he closed the cage.

"I'm intrigued, Markus. How did you acquire your delicious caramel colour?"

Markus was taken aback. "I guess you'd better ask my parents," he muttered feeling rather flustered.

Someone called out, "Gustav, stop flirting with the DJ!"

"Well?" asked Gustav. "I presume it wasn't just the sunbed."

"My father was Norwegian and my mother came from somewhere in Africa. I never knew her, though, as she was killed in some tribal war."

"Exotic *and* tragic," replied Gustav, smiling seductively. "I love it. You must come and join my little party."

"What about Frank? I can't leave him on his own!"

"Please don't worry your pretty little head. My boys will take care of him. And there's plenty of room here for both of you to stay overnight."

With that cleared up, there was little Markus could do to resist Gustav's entreaty so hand-in-hand they joined his party.

****

The screen showed a brief clip from Markus's pool-side set at Le Grand Macabre. The combination of his piano chops and the trance backing track was impressive and Frank was in his element, strutting his tiny, colourful stuff on top of the grand piano. The broadcast cut back to the *Breakfast* studio and the caption 'DJ Mista Mixa and Frank' appeared at the bottom of the screen. Markus was sitting on the vibrantly red sofa and was dressed in his trademark black outfit. His black T-shirt had a colourful, liquid crystal image of Frank on it. Markus looked bright-eyed and bushy-tailed despite the early hour. Frank was perched on his hand and his eyes were rotating madly. He didn't seem as vibrantly green as usual.

"Welcome to *Breakfast*, Markus and Frank," said Louise, one of the programme's presenters. "It must have been a hectic few weeks for the two of you; Ibiza one week and Dubai the next."

"It certainly has, Louise. I don't think our feet have hit the ground yet," replied Markus smiling.

"So Frank's a chameleon with an unusual appreciation of music," said Louise.

"That's right," replied Markus "He's a Jackson's chameleon and he changes colour with the beat."

"He looks as if he's just stepped off the set of *Jurassic Park*," added Charlie, the other presenter.

Markus laughed on cue. "Yes, males have three horns which make them look like a miniature triceratops."

"And I gather he's just enjoyed a breakfast on *Breakfast*," said Louise, bending over to cautiously stroke Frank's back.

"Yes, I gave him a few crickets and some water in the green room," replied Markus.

"And before Frank came into your life, I understand you were just a DJ trying to scrape together a living," explained Louise.

"That's right, Louise," replied Markus. "Somehow he rekindled my interest in the piano and boogie-woogie in particular."

"And you've developed a new genre: boogie-woogie trance, I gather," said Charlie.

Markus laughed engagingly. "I'm not sure I've developed anything new, really. It's just combining two things I love."

"And you've kindly agreed to play something for us this morning, I believe," said Louise, "but with Frank accompanying you."

Markus walked over to the grand piano to the left of the sofa and gently put Frank down on the lid. He sat down and started playing the bass line he'd used in his set at La Grand Macabre. Frank immediately perked up and colours rippled along his body. Markus added chords in his right hand that somehow managed to be both bluesy and trancey. Keeping the bass line going, he added in octaves in the left hand and leaps in the right hand. He looked up at Frank and noticed that one side of his body was drooping and turning brown. Seconds later, the other side of Frank's body went dark and he keeled over onto his side. Markus kept playing, trying to decide what to do. Frank's eyes had stopped moving and he didn't seem to be breathing. Markus half expected someone to shout out "Cut!" or whatever else they have to do to stop the cameras rolling. Tears welled up in the corners of his eyes and he realised he'd automatically changed how he was playing, the Rachmaninov virtuosity having morphed into something more akin to a Chopin nocturne. He looked again at Frank and knew for certain he was dead.

The *Breakfast* control room was trying to take all this in.

"Ideas?" asked the director, running his hands through what remained of his hair and watching Markus's tearful stoicism on the monitor.

"Well, he's busking like a pro, so I say let's see it out to the end," replied the assistant producer.

"Let's get a freeze from when the thing was still alive and add 'Frank RIP' at the bottom of the frame," said the director.

"What if it isn't dead?" asked someone else.

"Well, we'll all breathe a huge sigh of relief and apologise. If it's dead, we'll get a pat on the back for our quick thinking," replied the assistant director.

"Okay, let's run with it," said the director watching the feed from the camera focused on Markus. "Right, he's coming to the end... what's he saying?"

"It sounded like 'Goodbye, Frank' replied the assistant director.

"Okay, crossfade to the freeze and fade out," instructed the director. A brief moment of silence descended on the control room. "Brilliant, fucking brilliant," he said softly. "Okay, back to Louise and Charlie on the sofa... Oh, shit, they're crying..."

****

Roderick brushed away a tear. He closed the laptop but the final image of Frank collapsed on top of the piano stuck with him. *Did I contribute to Frank's death? Shit.* The doorbell pinged but he barely registered the sound. The next thing he knew there were two burly men with shaven heads and wearing ill-fitting white coats standing over him.

"We've come for the dog," one of them announced unpleasantly.

"And we don't want no trouble," said the other.

"What the fuck! Who the hell do you think you are?" said Roderick angrily. He stood up and was immediately pushed down by the men.

"It's the Official Secrets Act, mate. We've come to collect," said the first man.

"Over my dead body," retorted Roderick.

"If that's the way you want it...," said the second man menacingly who reached into his pocket for something.

Roderick didn't wait to find out what it was. Without realising exactly what he was doing, he projected his personas with an intensity and frequency he'd never attempted before. For the two men subjected to the barrage on their visual cortices it must have been like being caught in the centre of a boxing ring. The look in their eyes was one of horror and fear. Something liquid and yellow trickled onto the floor and pooled around their Doc Martens. Bruno was hiding in the corner watching the whole thing.

"Sod this. He can keep the fucking dog," said one of the men, making a run for the door.

"Wait for me!" called the other, following in quick pursuit.

It took Roderick some time to collect his thoughts. He felt as if he'd crossed a bridge with no way back, but he also didn't see the way forwards. He felt something nuzzling his leg and looked down to see Bruno gazing up at him. "Woof!" he went half-heartedly; he seemed shaken by what he'd witnessed.

"Christ, Bruno, what was all that about?"

Bruno looked imploringly and extended his paw. Roderick crouched down and took the paw in both hands.

"Don't worry, little chap. I'll keep you safe."

****

Frank's untimely death was greeted with the reverence expected for pop stars and other celebrities. Videos of his performances at Le Grand Macabre in Ibiza and the Chameleon Club in Dubai dominated TV channels, and interviews with pop pundits confirmed hyperbolically his legacy to the music industry. The clip from *Breakfast* went viral and was destined to go down in the annals of close encounters of the animal kind, surpassing even the defecating baby elephant in the *Blue Peter* studio. Although animal welfare experts were quick to criticise Frank's exploitation and suggested his death was due to stress, videos of the chameleon's vibrantly active last days suggested otherwise. The truth was he'd simply come to the end of the usual lifespan for a chameleon and at least he'd gone out with a bang.

Such was the outpouring of grief that Roderick and Markus decided Frank deserved a proper send-off rather than merely disposing of his tiny body. The Pet Cemetery in Islington was happy to provide their smallest coffin, giving Frank room to spare within the eighteen by twenty-four inch dimensions, and a humanist funeral celebrant was booked for the open-air service.

Markus's record label had ostentatiously provided a horse-drawn carriage and it was on a rather damp Friday morning that Markus and Roderick found themselves on the back seat in their suits with the utilitarian, council-supplied pet casket between them.

Roderick shook his head in disbelief at the sight of the cortège snaking into the distance behind the carriage. "This is surreal," he said, turning to look at Markus. "I can't believe we're about to bury a chameleon watched by a hundred mourners standing in the rain."

"I agree," replied Markus, "and there's still the a cappella singing to look forward to."

"You don't mean 'Karma Chameleon'?" asked Roderick, looking frankly horrified.

"I'm afraid so," replied Markus ruefully. "And with a quartet of singers all dressed up as chameleons. It wasn't my idea."

"So what will you do now Frank's no longer part of your act?"

"Well, a bit like Mikey and Sparky, it's been something of an epiphany for me. I'm no longer scared of using my classical training. But I can't see myself working with animals again. I'm going to be spending a lot of time in Germany."

"Is that because of Gustav?"

"Oh, you heard then? He's very exacting." He smiled as if recalling something pleasurable. "What about you? Back to business as usual?"

"Usual? I don't know what *usual* is these days. It was only last week that two men in white coats came into the shop intending to take Bruno back to god knows where. I asked them what the hell they were doing but they just quoted the Official Secrets Act. I got so pissed off that my shape-shifting went into overdrive and spooked them away. So, what with that, plus the publicity from Jeff, Cyril, and now Frank, perhaps I need to get back to simply running a pet shop."

"But why not capitalise on your talent at finding unusual pets? You could call it 'Exceptional Pets' or something. Be like Harrods used to be and offer to source rare and unusual animals."

"That's all very well but I don't think animal welfare would take kindly to a shape-shifter being in charge…"

Further discussion about Roderick's future came to a halt as soon as the carriage turned the corner. The grass verge outside the cemetery was covered with floral tributes and hundreds of well-wishers were lined up on the left waiting to be part of Frank's final journey. Some were dressed sombrely but most wore paraphernalia adorned with Frank's image. A handful were wearing chameleon costumes and there was also an eighties vintage, Boy George lookalike. The press were out in force and the paparazzi were ready to pounce on tearful prey with their telephoto lenses.

"Should we wave?" asked Markus, readying his hand.

"Probably not," replied Roderick. "We're hardly royals and this is meant to be a funeral after all."

"Well, I'm almost royal," corrected Markus. "Gustav and I are getting married in the summer."

"Okay, let's wave," agreed Roderick.

In fact, any semblance of dignity was destroyed by a garish floral construction in the approximate shape of a chameleon which had been fixed to the top of the carriage before the cortège got going. There was an equally tasteless 'Frank' tribute in front of it and both had flashing lights to hammer home the message that someone dear had departed.

The fellow mourners were standing around the tiny graveside by the time the carriage arrived with Markus, Roderick and the coffin. Against expectations, the humanist ceremony was remarkably free of pomp and circumstance. Markus delivered a tender and clearly heartfelt eulogy that managed to remain on the right side of the hyperbole that Frank had attracted in his short career in the music business. As the coffin was lowered into the grave, the mourners tossed dead crickets and snippets of vegetables onto the soil. True to Markus's word, the quartet of costumed singers did perform the unaccompanied version of 'Karma Chameleon'. Despite the words still making as little sense as they had back in the 80s, the song was strangely apt and moving. Roderick bent down and placed the regulation size plaque at the edge of the grave. Brian had written the epitaph. It wasn't exactly a haiku but it was near enough:

A tough little guy
He led life to the fullest
Boogie-woogie boy.

Chapter 6

Roderick

One chilly day in early December, Pete and Sam decided to pay Wet & Wild a visit as they were intrigued by the discrepancy in Roderick's appearance, and Sam had been giving more thought to the cast for his play. They had a pretext of buying some treats and a coat for Mr Choo to put under the Christmas tree. But there was also the issue of Sara Jane's unfortunate demise. They looked through the window first to make sure Cyril wasn't in his customary chair as neither relished a run-in with him again. When they entered the shop, Roderick was busy talking with a leggy blonde who was flirting with him. There was no doubt he had green eyes and long blond hair. This wasn't a look either of them would go for although it obviously appealed to the opposite sex. They took their time exploring the displays of dog treats and small dog coats, looking over every now and again to see whether the woman had left.

"Christ!" Pete exclaimed. "How the hell did he do that?"

"Do what?" replied Sam, who was fussing over a red tartan coat which purported to be 'traditional Royal Stewart Tartan' and had an appropriately north of the border price tag.

"Take a look yourself you dingbat," said Pete, irritated by Sam's devotion to all things dog.

Sam looked in Pete's direction and dropped the pile of tartan dog coats on the floor in amazement. Heading towards them was a drop-dead gorgeous man with grey eyes and dark hair.

"How are you getting on with the coats?" he asked with an enticing smile. "I see you found the tartan ones. They're on special offer at the moment, but they look better on a dog than on the floor." He bent down to help Sam pick up the coats and they locked eyes briefly.

"How the hell did you do that?" asked Pete incredulously, staring at the shop owner. "I mean, one minute you're blond and all but shagging that woman in front of us, and the next minute your hair has gone spiky and my boyfriend is all fingers and thumbs and can't keep his eyes off you."

"And obviously has lustful ideas," replied Roderick looking at Sam's jeans, "assuming that isn't really a banana in his pocket."

Sam blushed. "Sorry," he said, instantly deflated.

"Well, I suppose I owe you some sort of explanation," said Roderick. "To put it simply, I'm two non-identical twins in the same body."

"You mean a split personality?" Pete asked.

"A bit more than that," explained Roderick. "It's more like having two fully formed people inside me and I can choose which one people see."

"That's molto bizarro, man, and more than a tad creepy," said Pete. "Can you prove it?"

"Easy," said Roderick. He briefly closed his eyes in concentration and then opened them again. This time, they were green and his face had morphed along with his hair colour. He did the same thing again and switched seemingly effortlessly back to his grey-eyed, dark-haired persona.

Sam and Pete looked at each other, mouths open in amazement, not daring to believe what they'd just witnessed. "Wow and double wow!" Sam exclaimed.

"That's awesome, man," agreed Pete. "Can you do anything else?"

"Well, I can sort of disappear," said Roderick.

"You mean with a cloaking device like the Klingons?" Sam asked.

"Not exactly," replied Roderick. "Give me a minute and I'll show you. In the meantime, keep looking at the dog coats."

Sam and Pete returned to examining the items on the rack and Roderick walked to the back of the shop. He quietly removed his clothes and stood naked for about 30 seconds, allowing his breathing to slow right down and concentrating on blocking any individuality. He slowly walked to the front of the shop and stood about two feet away from Sam and Pete who were oblivious of his presence and talking about him.

"If he can do that with his face, what do you think he can do with his dick?" Pete asked.

"You mean, like turn it into a John Holmes replica that both of us can enjoy at the same time," said Sam.

"Frigging hell!" exclaimed Pete.

"More like frigging heaven, I'd say!" retorted Sam. They giggled.

Roderick inwardly chuckled being careful to keep his guard up, and walked to the back of the shop where he put his clothes back on. He returned again to where Pete and Sam were waiting for him.

"Hey, man," said Pete impatiently, "we're still waiting for the vanishing trick."

Roderick smiled. "It's already happened. I walked right up to you."

"You're joking!" exclaimed Pete.

"I'm not. You were talking about me and specifically about my John Thomas."

"Oops," said Sam blushing.

"Er, I think you mean John Holmes," said Pete.

"And I was in the buff," said Roderick.

"You mean there was a naked guy a few feet away from us and we didn't see him?" Pete asked with astonishment.

"That about sums it up," replied Roderick. "I'll show you the security video that was recording at the time." Roderick led them to a laptop next to the till and selected something with the touchpad. The three of them watched as the segment of video played. Sam and Pete saw themselves standing in front of a display rack at the front of the shop and they were talking about something. A man walked into view from the back of the shop and there wasn't a jot of clothing on him. Apart from that there was nothing remarkable about him. It wasn't obvious whether his hair was light or dark. The man stood a few feet away from Sam and Pete and then retraced his steps back to where he'd come from. Roderick watched their reaction with amusement.

"Hot diggity damn!" said Pete, looking flabbergasted. "That wasn't actually you, was it?"

"Definitely me," said Roderick.

"But he didn't look like you," said Sam. "In fact, he didn't look like anybody, really."

"That's half the secret," said Roderick. "If you're physically unremarkable and think yourself into having zero presence, you've got the start of an invisibility cloak."

"Jeez," exclaimed Pete. "So it's not exactly like twitching your nose or waving a wand. But it sure must make your life complicated."

"It does," agreed Roderick. "Running the pet shop is plain sailing as the animals don't mind what I look like as long as I smell the same and feed them at the right time."

"That reminds me," said Sam, "We couldn't help notice that Cyril wasn't in his usual place. What's happened to him?"

"Ah," said Roderick with an audible sigh. "Unfortunately, after he was returned to the shop by the RSPCA, things didn't quite work out. In fact, it all became very difficult. He was very hungry but wouldn't touch his usual dry food and only sniffed at wet cat food. It seems he was missing Sara Jane for more than the reason of her company."

"That's sick!" Sam exclaimed.

"That's cats for you," said Roderick. "We like to think they're happy eating manufactured food but give them a taste of the real stuff and they know what they prefer."

"What happened next?" Pete asked.

"Well he lost weight, which was a good thing, but the claws also came out. At least I could escape at night and the invisibility cloak helped a bit, but the other animals weren't so fortunate. In the end we had to let him go, although the vet said his heart would have packed up anytime soon."

"So he was euthanised, then?" Pete asked.

"That's the expression vets use these days," said Roderick, "although I don't think the average pet owner likes it."

"Perhaps we ought to euthanise Mr Choo," said Sam mischievously.

"Just you try it!" Pete said defensively. He turned back to Roderick. "Sorry, but my boyfriend and my dog don't get on together."

"Well, I suppose the Chihuahua is an acquired taste," said Roderick. "Take the Tibetan terrier for example…'

And before Roderick could finish the sentence, Sam and Pete noticed a dog calmly walk across the ceiling and then down the wall head first. Back safely on the ground, the dog looked up at them expectantly, wagging its stumpy tail.

"What the hell…?" exclaimed Sam and Pete in disbelief.

"Ah," replied Roderick, "that's the Tibetan terrier I was about to compare with a Chihuahua. As you can see, he's an active dog but his temperament is easy-going and he's very good at playing fetch. He's just been returned to the shop after an unfortunate accident."

"But how…?" Pete started to ask.

Roderick completed the question, "How does he climb walls? Well I *could* tell you but you'd have to sign the Official Secrets Act."

Sam and Pete looked at each other, unsure what to say.

"Sorry, I was pulling your leg," Roderick said smiling. "Actually, he's got gecko footpads which allow him to stick to walls. I did sell him but his owner didn't follow my instructions and he ended up with a broken leg after gravity got the better of him."

Sam got his voice back. "Do you have any other surprises in store? Like a snake that can whistle, for instance?"

"Sorry, no," replied Roderick. "I sold Peter last week."

Pete was tugging at Sam's arm. "I think we should leave, sweetie."

"There was one thing I wanted to ask you about," said Sam. "Pete mentioned that you used to act."

"Yes, I went to drama school just down the road," replied Roderick. "In fact, I've still got my Equity card."

"That's interesting. I might be in touch. Thanks, Roderick."

Roderick shook hands with Sam and Pete and they left the shop. Brian came out of hiding. "So you've got two new boyfriends now," he said smirking.

"Very funny," replied Roderick.

"So why did you walk up to them naked then?"

"You were watching?"

"If you ask me, it's a bit pervy walking around naked."

"Well, I'm not asking you." Roderick turned back to the desk.

Brian sneered, "You know how good I am with YouTube." He walked off.

Shit, thought Roderick. That was a good example why he shouldn't let his guard down. He'd made an exhibition of himself which was precisely the sort of idiotic behaviour that got him into trouble at drama school. Come to think of it, why had Sam asked him about acting?

Sam and Pete were walking back home from the pet shop. "Is he always like that?" asked Pete.

"Like what?" Sam replied.

"You know, taking the piss."

"Actually, I don't think he was. I think he's dead serious."

"Well, part of him may be dead gorgeous but I'm not sure about serious. So do you think he'd be suitable for your play?"

"Well, it's probably a long shot, but I think it might just work after seeing that incredible demonstration…"

****

Roderick finally got around to checking his emails. The day had been difficult – largely because Brian was being more perverse than usual and quite literally driving Bruno up the wall. He scanned the subject lines and noticed one that stood out because it read 'Dinner chez nous?' Given that he'd made such an ass of himself he hadn't expected to hear from Pete and Sam again. As well as suggesting a meal at theirs, Sam wanted to discuss an 'opportunity' which had arisen. Roderick checked dates and saw that the suggested assignation was tomorrow. His first reaction was to politely decline but a niggling thought prompted him to accept the invitation. Sam and Pete had given their full names at the bottom of the email and he couldn't resist searching their names on Google – an act which Brian would doubtless read far too much into. His heart skipped a beat when he found references to Sam as a 'visiting playwright' at the London Metropolitan University. He considered digging out the script of *Rosencrantz and Guildenstern Are Dead* to demonstrate he could play two parts, but decided that was being rash and he'd probably just make a Shakespearian fool of himself anyway.

Rather too much like a star-crossed lover, he was also being idiotically indecisive about what to wear to dinner, so in the end he simply wore jeans and a T-shirt. As soon as he put a foot on the steps leading down to Sam and Pete's apartment he heard a shrill bark emanating from inside. A tiny dog appeared at speed from around the corner, yapped at him like a demented machine gun and then disappeared through a door flap. Roderick liked dogs, but he liked them even more if they had a sense of decorum.

He heard Sam calling out behind him as he opened the front door: "That frigging mutt. He'll end up in the curry if he's not careful!" He turned around and noticed Roderick standing at the doorstep. "Oh, sorry, Roderick. He's been so hyper since Sara Jane's death. Anyway, it's good to see you again. Come on in."

"He's probably feeling insecure," Roderick said as he entered the apartment. "Perhaps he's worried something will happen to you."

Sam laughed. "That'd be the day, but I have to admit I don't understand dogs. That's Pete's territory."

"What's my territory?" Pete asked, emerging from the kitchen with Mr Choo following closely behind. The dog started yapping again as soon as he saw Roderick. "Shush!" Pete said, admonishing the dog. "Be nice to our guest."

Roderick bent down and placed a package on the floor. "I've got a peace offering for him." The dog came forward nervously and sniffed at whatever was wrapped up. He wagged his tail.

"Treats?" Pete asked.

"Plus the red tartan dog coat you seemed so keen on. I hope it fits," replied Roderick who stood up and handed the package to Pete.

"Wow, that's sweet of you," said Pete. "You deserve a hug for that."

The two of them hugged and Sam joined in. Roderick realised too late the close physical contact had triggered a momentary shimmering. "You did something rather strange then," said Pete, who was looking at Roderick's face from about a foot away. "The only way I can describe it is a shifting of your features. It only lasted a moment but I'm sure something happened."

"I agree," said Sam, who was staring with fascination at Roderick's face. Roderick blushed and realised he was powerless to stop another bout of shimmering. Sam and Pete watched transfixed. "That's astonishing," said Sam. "It's as if you were about to slide into another dimension."

"Does that mean you're actually a shape-shifter?" asked Pete.

"Well, I suppose I'm the nearest there is to such a thing, but I can't take on the appearance of anyone or anything I come into contact with," replied Roderick. "Not that I'd want to turn into a Chihuahua anyway."

"Good point," said Sam. "Let's see how the coat fits." He unwrapped the parcel and between the two of them, Sam and Pete managed to get the dog into the coat with the minimum of yelps.

"Perfect," he said, looking at the ridiculous dog in the equally ridiculous coat. "What do you think, love?" he asked Pete.

"I agree," replied Pete. "He's quite the dandy now." He bent down and offered the dog a handful of treats which were devoured instantly. "I'd better get back to the kitchen before it all burns. You two can talk while I'm finishing the cooking. It's all vegetarian, by the way."

Sam and Roderick sat down. Sam was still examining Roderick's face intently. "I still don't understand how you can do the face changing thing. Your face looks so normal on the surface."

"I can't say I fully understand myself," said Roderick. "And as you saw, my control over it goes to pieces sometimes."

"What about if you were on stage?" Sam asked.

"That's different, I think," Roderick replied. "If I'm playing a part that suits a persona then the projection is reinforced. Where it falls apart is when there's a mismatch or if I'm distracted in some way. For example, I did a stand-up act in a mime festival recently which was a disaster because of hecklers in the audience."

"Does close physical contact have the same effect?"

"Exactly. And that's why relationships are a nightmare for me."

"So, if you don't mind me asking, are you gay or straight?"

"No, that's okay, but it's complicated. Basically, one twin is gay and the other is straight."

"You're bi, then?"

"Sort of but not really. That's why physical contact is difficult. The gay twin obviously likes physical contact with other guys but the straight one doesn't. And vice versa with women. I think that's why the shimmering happens."

"Interesting," said Sam thoughtfully. "It must make your love life hell."

Roderick grinned ruefully. "That's why it's almost non-existent. Still, I'm always hoping something might change for the better."

There was the sound of something clanging on the kitchen floor followed by a sharp yelp from Mr Choo. "Sorry!" called out Pete.

"So, going back to the theatre, have you ever played more than one character in a production?" asked Sam.

"Like the leads in *Rosencrantz and Guildenstern Are Dead*, you mean?" Sam nodded. "Yes, my year did that as our graduation piece, but it was so subtly lit I don't think the audience was aware of what I was doing."

"And you managed to keep in part for the two hours?"

"I think so. And I also managed to pull off the two characters disappearing at the end of the third act."

"You know, Roderick, I think we could–"

Pete called from the kitchen, "Dinner's ready!"

"We'll talk more after dinner," Sam said mysteriously.

Pete had prepared a range of Indian vegetarian dishes with an aromatic vegetarian biryani as the centrepiece. "Help yourself," he said to Roderick.

"This looks so good and just what I needed after a hard day in the pet shop," said Roderick.

"Is it hard work?" asked Sam.

"Well, not really," admitted Roderick. "Much of it is tedious, but you never know who's going to walk through the door or what animal is going to turn up."

"You certainly go for unusual pets," said Pete.

"I guess it's because I have an affinity with anything that's unusual," said Roderick.

"But aren't you exploiting them a bit?" Sam asked.

"I don't deny it," replied Roderick, "but charity comes into it as well – animals no one else wants, for instance."

"Like Cyril, you mean," said Pete.

Roderick looked at Pete directly. "Well, our intentions with him were good – and I did invest quite a lot in his upkeep, after all – but it's impossible to cover all eventualities. It never dawned on me Sara Jane would allow herself to be manipulated by Cyril in the way she was. And I did offer her help if she wanted it."

"We did as well, but it's hard not to feel a bit guilty when something as awful as that happens," said Sam.

"So, how actually was Cyril able to get inside my mind?" Pete asked, still trying to get over the experience.

"To be honest, I don't know," replied Roderick. "If I said he used ESP that begs the question what ESP is, and most people don't even believe in ESP. I tried to discuss Cyril's ability with vets but they didn't take me seriously and thought I was a nut."

"Are there any more like him?" Sam asked.

"I guess it's possible," replied Roderick. "He was a cross between Maine Coon and Savannah and must have been one of a litter. His previous owner was an elderly lady, but I don't know how he came into her life."

"Does being obese have anything to do with the ESP thing?" Pete asked.

"That had occurred to me," replied Roderick. "I suppose it could be a self-preservation mechanism which kicks in when an animal gets too big to hunt food for itself."

"You mean, like the animal ordering a takeaway?" suggested Sam.

They laughed. "Something like that, I guess," replied Roderick. "So, tell me a bit about yourselves. How did you meet?"

Sam and Pete exchanged a glance. "Well, we were both out jogging on a track back in Vancouver," said Pete.

"You know, the passing glance followed by a count to two and then a look behind," added Sam. "So we broke off our jogs and had sex in the bushes."

"That was five years ago," added Pete. "And there's been no sex in the bushes since."

The three of them laughed. "And how come you're in London?" Roderick asked.

"For artistic pursuits really," replied Sam. "Pete is studying sculpture at Saint Martins and I write and direct plays. Vancouver is good for the arts but London is better. Also, I was offered a position as visiting playwright with the London Metropolitan University."

Roderick knew about the latter from his research but wasn't going to let on. "Does that have something to do with what you wanted to discuss?"

Sam and Pete looked at each other. "Go on, love. Tell him," said Pete.

"Well…," said Sam hesitantly. "Okay, Roderick. This is the score. I'd like you to be in a play I've written. In fact, you'd be playing not one but three parts."

Roderick was open-mouthed. "But are you sure? You haven't even seen me act yet."

"We've seen what you can do with your, er, *ability* and that's enough to make me think the play would work. It'd be very experimental and we'd have to use video projection and cut-out doubles to add to the visual interest, but I think it's worth a go."

Roderick still looked stunned and a bit of shimmering gave away his emotional reaction. "Gosh, I don't know what to say."

"Yes?" suggested Pete.

"Well, yes, of course," said Roderick. "I suppose I should add that I'll need to check with my agent but actually she gave up on me years ago."

"That's fantastic," said Sam. "Let's finish eating and then we can arrange to meet so I can give you the script and tell you more about the play."

Mr Choo took that opportunity to dive through the flap in the kitchen door. In fact, they hadn't registered he'd been elsewhere while they were eating. The dog coat was partially undone and had picked up some dirt on his travels. He had something in his mouth and was clearly intent on extracting the maximum enjoyment from whatever he was chewing. Pete bent down and put out his hand. The Chihuahua warned him off with a growl from deep within its scrawny throat. "What've you got there, you silly thing?" Pete asked. The dog growled again more insistently. Pete could see the end of the object protruding from the dog's mouth. "Oh my god!" he said, looking utterly aghast.

"What is it?" Sam asked, turning to look at what their pet was up to.

"Look at what's in Mr Choo's mouth!" Pete said. "Fuck! I think it's a finger!"

Sam and Pete knelt on the floor and between the two of them managed to extract the object from between the dog's teeth. Roderick came around to assist with inspecting the object. "Jesus! You're right! You can even see nail varnish!"

All three of them looked ashen. "Are you thinking what I'm thinking?" asked Pete.

"Sara Jane?" replied Sam.

"Oh fuck!" said Pete.

"I think we should call the police," said Sam. "After all, it could be someone else's finger. Pete, you go ring 999 and I'll put the finger in a plastic bag."

****

Roderick left before the police arrived. They hadn't felt like returning to their food after Mr Choo's surprise delivery. Although no one actually voiced the thought, all three felt that Sara Jane was somehow pointing a finger from beyond the grave.

Despite the unexpectedly gruesome end to the evening, Roderick felt elated. He also had the sort of quivery feeling he associated with a first date, although the Chihuahua's appearance with the finger was a more likely explanation for the nauseous foreboding. He couldn't stop himself shimmering. He was sure people passing by must have noticed something strange about him although no one was staring.

****

Roderick had arranged to meet with Sam in the theatre school's coffee bar just after the shop closed. He'd prepared a couple of scenes from *Rosencrantz and Guildenstern Are Dead* in case Sam wanted him to audition. In the student production of the play, the director achieved the character switch by having him look right or left with a tight spotlight on his face and he wasn't sure how it would work without the lighting.

"Hi, Sam," Roderick said, joining Sam at the counter. "Thanks for an almost perfect evening."

"It was our pleasure," said Sam, shaking hands. "Pete enjoys practising his culinary skills. It was such a shame about the macabre interruption."

"So, what did the police say?"

"Well, they haven't taken Mr Choo in for questioning yet. But as they say, hope springs eternal. The police came back the following morning with a sniffer dog that led them right back to Sara Jane's flat. They think they'll be able to match the finger Mr Choo found with the bit of finger Cyril regurgitated, although it may have already been cremated with the body."

"Christ! Cyril certainly bit off a lot more than he could chew." Roderick shuddered. "What a horrible thought."

Sam nodded. "Anyway, let's grab some coffees and I'll take you to a room we use for read-throughs."

"Would you like me to audition?" asked Roderick as they were walking. "I've prepared a couple of scenes just in case."

"That would be helpful but don't feel you have to impress too much. It's all work in progress at the moment."

They reached the room and sat down. "Right, let me tell you about the play," said Sam. "The working title is 'Tx', which is the medical abbreviation for therapy, treatment and also transplant. There are three characters: a therapist and two non-identical twins, one of whom is gay and the other is straight. The therapist knows they're twins and has to maintain confidentiality about him seeing both of them. They've always been rivals and the therapist believes this has culminated in murderous fantasies about killing each other. To complicate matters the therapist has developed erotic fantasies about the twins having an incestuous relationship. He knows he should call a halt to the therapy but can't because he's feeding off the fantasies. In fact, they've known all along that each other is seeing the therapist. They end up killing the therapist to silence him and then go off to continue their incestuous relationship."

"Wow, that's quite a story," said Roderick, who'd been listening to the synopsis in goggle-eyed amazement. "How much was written after you met me for the first time in the pet shop?"

"Actually, very little of it," Sam replied. "Although I've obviously had to make changes so you could play all three parts. It's based on a true life story of twins who murdered their therapist after he discovered a little too much about them."

"How do you see the shifting between the twins working?"

"Well, some scenes would have the twins on opposite sides of the stage. For example, while the gay twin goes off cruising on Hampstead Heath, the straight one is watching porn on a laptop. We'd have to work out the transitions. That's where projection and cut-outs might be used. It's all smoke and mirrors really. Then right at the end, the two of you would join together in the middle just as if you're actually having sex."

"Would you want me naked?"

"I'm not sure yet. What happens to the twins when they're naked?"

"That's a good question. Fully clothed, I've a complete awareness of my body from head to toe. So, if I was naked and switched with my twin, I'm fairly sure you'd see a full transformation rather than just my head. We can try it out if you want."

"I can't wait to see," said Sam with a grin, "although perhaps Pete should be here as a chaperone."

Roderick laughed. "Yes, that might be wise."

"Would you like to do your audition piece now?"

"Okay. I'm doing the start of Act One of *Rosencrantz and Guildenstern Are Dead*." Roderick put his hand in a pocket and extracted a coin. "This is my prop." He sat down on a chair about six feet away from Sam, looked to the right and then tossed the coin and said, "Heads."

As soon as Roderick started, Sam could see his choice of play was inspired. Rosencrantz and Guildenstern were frequently seen as two halves of a single character and here was an actor demonstrating exactly that just a few feet away from him. But it was a bizarre experience seeing someone morph into a different person simply by turning his head one way or the other. Sam found himself trying to see behind the illusion as his brain was struggling to process how Roderick achieved the transformation without some sleight of hand. It was also clear Roderick possessed a remarkable ability at timing which suited the sparseness of the opening of the play. Sam had looked up reviews of the student production Roderick had been part of and it was obvious critics hadn't appreciated the full extent of Roderick's talent. Neither had they cottoned on to his shape-shifting ability. He was definitely wasted as the owner of a pet shop. Roderick came to the end of the audition piece and then looked straight ahead at Sam, morphing into the bland, unremarkable, in-between version of himself.

Sam drew a breath. "Phew, that was extraordinary!"

"You liked it?" asked Roderick who'd switched back to the grey-eyed, dark-haired twin.

"Did I like it? It was incredible!" Sam got up and walked across to Roderick to give him a hug. He looked at his face. "You didn't shimmer that time."

Roderick smiled. "That's probably because I'm getting used to your hugs."

"You know, I still don't understand how you pull off the shape-shifting. I was convinced there were two characters sitting on the chair and I wanted to work out the trick."

"But that's good. An illusion is a lot less threatening than the real thing."

Sam nodded. "And the real thing would be the discovery that someone can manipulate your mind without you knowing it."

"Which would be pretty frightening for most people."

"So, you wouldn't mind if we used an element of illusion in the play on top of what you can do?"

"Not at all. I think it should help with pulling off something that's more audacious – like the ending, for instance."

"Yes, I was thinking of that when you came to the end of the audition piece. I was wondering how fast you can switch between characters."

"You mean between the twins?"

"Yes, but also including yourself without the twins' features."

"I'm not sure. It takes a bit of concentration to make the switch but I'll have a go."

Sam walked to the back of the room and watched as Roderick briefly closed his eyes and then changed into the green-eyed, blond-haired twin. The process took a few seconds, which Sam thought might be a bit slow to achieve the impact he was hoping for in the final scene. Roderick then switched back to the dark-haired twin and seemed able to do this without closing his eyes this time. As the sequence continued, it was clear Roderick was gaining control of the shape-shifting, with the transition between the twins taking barely a second. Finally, he shifted to his in-between self just as he'd done in the audition. Sam clapped and Roderick gave a deep bow.

"That's stunning, Roderick. With the right lighting, the ending should be sensational. It also helps seeing you from a distance. How do you feel trying that without any clothing?"

"Now?"

"If that's okay with you. I'll stay here, so it's definitely hands off."

Roderick laughed. "Okey-dokey, Mr Director." Roderick undressed unselfconsciously, as if he'd been expecting to be asked.

"Standing up or sitting down?"

"Standing up, I think," replied Sam.

As Roderick had said earlier, there was absolutely no doubt his awareness of the twins extended from head to toe. Subtle differences in the twins' bodies made the shape-shifting even more impressive than before. The dark-haired twin had appropriately dark hair on his well-defined body, whereas the blond-haired one had a smoother, less toned appearance. The slight reservation Sam had was that the naked spectacle was harder to explain as an illusion.

"Roderick, could you move a bit? Perhaps you could crouch down and then stand up and also turn around." Roderick nodded and crouched down. Suddenly, his body lost cohesion and almost vanished. Roderick reappeared as the dark-haired twin with a puzzled expression on his face and rubbing his head.

"Sorry, I'm not sure what happened there. I'd probably been pushing myself too hard."

"Jeez, that really was like something out of H. G. Wells. Are you okay, though?"

"Yes, I'm fine. My body didn't actually start to disappear. It must have been the invisibility cloak kicking in when I wasn't expecting it. Maintaining control over the changes has always been the problem for me." Roderick started putting his clothes back on.

"Has that happened on stage?"

Roderick nodded. "Funnily enough it didn't happen with *Rosencrantz and Guildenstern*. It usually occurred when I had a small part and was getting bored. Again, no one realised what had actually happened, but the audience was aware of something and I got accused of trying to upstage the cast's leads."

Sam laughed. "I'm not at all surprised. It must have been very disconcerting. So is that why you stopped acting?"

"One of the reasons. I also felt like doing something different with more routine and better pay."

"Don't I know it! That's the unhappy mantra of all struggling actors. But not many go on to run a pet shop."

Sam started gathering up papers. "Okay, Roderick, I think that's everything for today."

Roderick looked anxious. "Have I got the part?"

"Of course you have. And I'm looking forward to working with you. Do you have any questions?"

"Do you have a date and venue arranged yet? Also, when would rehearsals start?"

"Right. I'm thinking four weeks rehearsal starting first thing in the New Year and I've booked a week in the studio theatre here for the first week in February. It seats a maximum of 150 and can be reconfigured for in the round and with variable degrees of rake. How does that sound to you?"

"Will that give enough time for the production design?"

"It should do. I've already lined up some techie whizz-kids and they're itching to get started. Which reminds me, presumably when we video you it'll only record the basic you, like the video we saw in the pet shop."

"That's right. I can only manipulate the mind, not technology. So there'd be no point in videoing me as you see me now or as the other twin."

"But we could video what you call the 'in-between' version of yourself."

"Yes, that would work. Were you thinking of using that version for the therapist?"

"That's the plan. I'm hoping to use something called a 'virtual mannequin', which involves a video of someone projected onto a life-size, transparent cut-out of their body. It'd solve the problem of showing a twin on stage with the therapist at the same time. I also like the idea of making the therapist so detached he's actually disembodied."

"It all sounds really impressive. I just hope I don't make a mess of it. You're putting a lot of faith in me, Sam."

"I'm sure it'll work. And remember you'll be acting alongside video, so that should take some pressure off the live performance. As far as rehearsals are concerned, we'll try to fit in with your schedule. Do you think your assistant could run the shop some days?"

"I'll speak with him. Sales might suffer, but it's about time he was unleashed on the unsuspecting public."

Sam extracted a loosely bound stack of paper from his leather satchel. "Here's the script. Don't take too much notice of the directions. Would this Friday be good for the read-through?"

Roderick took the script and quickly thumbed through it. "Friday is usually a quiet day anyway. I'll check first thing tomorrow and let you know."

"That's great, Roderick. I've got a good feeling about this project."

Roderick was about to leave when Sam asked him, "By the way, do you have names for the twins?"

"Not really, as they're both part of me," Roderick replied, "But I suppose you could call them 'Rod' and 'Rick' if that helps."

"Well, I've put 'gay twin' and 'straight twin' in the script for the time being. I'd considered putting 'dark hair' and 'blond hair' but one or both of the twins might have a makeover before the play opens."

Roderick laughed.

****

Roderick felt almost exhilarated when he got back home. It wasn't entirely a good feeling as there was a little too much trepidation for it to be a hundred per cent positive. It was liberating to give full vent to his shape-shifting ability but he was also aware of the dangers of not being fully in control. The notion of taking to the stage for what was effectively a one-man show would have seemed ludicrous just a few weeks ago – particularly after the disaster of his attempt at doing mime.

There were many aspects to Sam's play which appealed to him. Standing naked in front of an audience wasn't one of them but it didn't make him particularly anxious either. He wasn't sure he'd want his parents in the audience, though. But the opportunity for the twins to work through their rivalry in front of an audience was what intrigued him most. And he couldn't believe the play had been adapted specifically for him.

He Googled the names of the twins involved in the original murder and discovered the case involved conjoined twins separated by surgery, who couldn't cope with being more than inches apart. They developed intrusive thoughts about taking revenge on the surgical team and were referred to the therapist. The account of what then happened made for macabre reading and he wondered how his twins would have coped with surgical separation.

The following morning he made a point of collecting two coffees before heading for the shop. He needed to discuss rehearsal time with Brian.

Brian slouched into the shop ten minutes late. Roderick almost said, "Boyfriend trouble?" but thought better of it. His attempts at humour with Brian always fell flat. He proffered the rapidly cooling cup of coffee. "Sorry, it's got a bit cold."

Brian looked at the cup in Roderick's hand, uncertain whether to take it. "What's it for?" he asked.

"Well, we normally drink it," Roderick replied, immediately regretting the sarcasm.

Brian took the cup in his hand but still looked suspicious. "Why the coffee?" he asked more directly.

"I need to talk with you about something," said Roderick ominously.

Brian's hackles rose dramatically. "What d'you mean? Have I done something wrong?"

Roderick held out his hands to placate him. "No, Brian, you've done nothing wrong. In fact, I'm very pleased with your work. The thing is–"

"–You can't afford to pay me," Brian interrupted.

Roderick sighed. This wasn't going well. "No, Brian, that's not it," he said patiently. He had to come out with it. "The thing is I've got a part in a play."

Brian's mouth had dropped open. "You're an actor?" he asked unbelievingly.

"Yes, I was," Roderick replied. "I mean I am."

Brian's mouth seemed reluctant to close.

"And that means there'll be days when I'll be rehearsing and you'll need to look after the shop," Roderick added. "I'll put your pay up, of course."

Brian was clearly finding this about-turn in his employment situation too much to take in.

"I know it's a lot to ask of you. Do you think you can manage that?" asked Roderick.

Just then the ping of the doorbell announced the presence of a customer. Pete walked in carrying a cage with a purple cover. He looked flustered. "I'm really sorry to spring this on you, Roderick, but I didn't know who else to turn to." He took the cover off the cage to reveal an adult parrot Roderick recognised as an African Grey. "Sam and I agreed to look after him for a couple of actor friends who've decamped to Gran Canaria for Christmas, but he's been driving Mr Choo insane. It'll only be for a couple of weeks. We'd pay for board and lodging, of course."

"What do you think, Brian?" said Roderick, suddenly realising Brian had retreated to the back of the shop. He turned back to Pete. "Sorry, Pete, I just wanted to check with my assistant." He walked over to inspect the parrot. "He's certainly a beauty. What's his name?"

"What a gay day," said the parrot in a passable imitation of the dead, stand-up comedian Larry Grayson. The parrot cast his beady eyes over Roderick. "Ooh, look at his bona basket."

Pete looked embarrassed. "I'm afraid he's a rather camp parrot. He's picked up his owners' bitching plus stuff from old TV and radio shows."

"Get that homy polone," the bird added with a queeny fluff of his feathers.

"I don't believe it!" exclaimed Roderick, trying to stifle his laughter. "He's fantastic."

"Shut that door!" the bird said with appropriate finality.

Roderick and Pete were practically doubled up with laughter.

"We'd be honoured to have him stay in our humble B&B," Roderick said after recovering from his mirth. "So what *is* his name?"

"It's 'JG'," replied Pete, "after John Gielgud."

"Dear, dear Johnny," added the parrot in an actorly tone, "I knew him well."

"Brian!" Roderick called. "Come and say hello to JG."

Brian emerged uncertainly from the shadows. His eyes lit up like neon lights as soon as he saw the parrot. "Wow, an African Grey. My aunt has one just like him." He waggled a tempting finger near the bars of the cage.

JG inspected Brian's finger haughtily, as if scrutinising a dubious morsel of food, and inclined his head towards Pete. "Seems like a nice boy," he said and then added a throaty cackle for good effect.

"Brian, could you settle him in and give him something to eat?" asked Roderick. "We should have some parrot food in the bird seed section."

Brian took the cage over to the far corner of the shop where the parrot would still be seen but hopefully not over-stimulated. Brian and JG could be heard jousting with scabrous insults and the parrot seemed to be winning.

"Sam was very impressed by your audition yesterday," Pete said.

"Really?" said Roderick.

"And I gather he didn't waste any time getting you undressed," Pete added sarcastically.

Roderick blushed.

"Don't worry. I know it was entirely innocent," said Pete smiling. "Although I wouldn't have minded being there," he added with an exaggerated lick of the lips.

****

"Break a leg!" squawked JG as Roderick left the pet shop for the university's theatre school the following Friday. He wasn't sure whether a random parrot utterance counted as a bona fide good luck wish. When he arrived for the read-through he was startled to find four other people present in the room in addition to Sam, and he wondered whether the parrot might have been unusually prescient after all.

"Roderick, would you mind doing the opening scene from *Rosencrantz and Guildenstern* again?" asked Sam. "These guys aren't convinced you'll be able to pull off all the parts yourself, so I thought it'd help them to see what you did in the audition. I'll then get them to introduce themselves."

"No problem, Sam. I'd be happy to." Roderick extracted a coin from his wallet. He sat down on a chair, looked to the right and then tossed the coin and said, "Heads."

Sam watched the expressions on the faces of his four colleagues as Roderick morphed between the two characters. If anything, the transitions seemed slicker this time, although there were occasions when Roderick lingered for a moment before the change, almost as if making a point about the characters being inseparable. At the end of the excerpt, he stared straight ahead and allowed the twins to retreat into the background.

"Does anyone have any questions?" Sam asked, addressing his evidently overawed colleagues.

A dark-haired woman immediately to Sam's right was the first to say something. She'd been staring intently at Roderick throughout the excerpt. "I'm Sally, production design.

Roderick, that was utterly extraordinary. It's obviously an illusion but I don't see how you're doing it."

Roderick looked at Sam who nodded. "Okay...," he said. He took a deep breath. "I'm what's known as a genetic chimera." He paused and looked at the newcomers to see whether that meant anything. He continued, "I was born with two non-identical twins inside me and they're most developed in my brain. Somehow I can use my mind to make people believe they're seeing one or the other twin. Sometimes both twins try to make themselves seen and that's when you might notice me shimmering. If I concentrate, I can also push both twins into the background and people see a raw, undifferentiated me."

"So there's actually no trick," said Sally, looking flabbergasted. "It's really you doing it!"

"That's about it," Roderick confirmed. "Also, if I relax very deeply, it can appear I'm not there – almost as if I'm wearing an invisibility cloak – but it's not easy to pull that off reliably."

"Does it matter if you've got a spotlight on you?" asked a large, bearded man next to Sally. "I'm Geoff, lighting design, by the way."

"Not really," replied Roderick. "If anything, a spotlight helps, as the twins seem to enjoy being in the limelight on their own – particularly the gay one." His small audience laughed.

A woman on Sam's left was next to ask a question. "Hi, Roderick. I'm Jemma, Sam's assistant. I'm wondering about the size of the audience. Is there any difference for you between a room with just five people and an auditorium of four hundred?"

Roderick looked thoughtful. "Well, the simple answer is I don't know. I'd imagine the closer the audience is to me, the stronger the effect. Also, like hypnosis, it probably depends a lot on suggestibility.

"But the studio theatre here should be all right for you?" asked Sam.

"I think so," Roderick replied, "but we should try it out sooner rather than later."

"Agreed, we'll arrange that for next week," said Sam

A geeky-looking man with glasses to Jemma's left put up his hand. "I'm Clive. I'll be doing the video. Excuse my bluntness, but what would I actually record if I pointed a camera at you?"

Roderick looked at Sam. "Shall I show him?"

Sam nodded.

They watched as Roderick stared ahead appearing to concentrate. He morphed from the handsome, dark-haired twin, who seemed just as real as themselves, to a man of roughly the same age whose predominant characteristic was blandness. He was neither good-looking nor ugly, and if asked, they wouldn't have been able to describe his hair or eye colour. And as they watched, his features became even more indistinct, his skin and hair colour becoming imperceptible from the surroundings of the room. They blinked, hardly wanting to trust their eyes, but when they looked again, Roderick was back as the dark-haired twin. There was a collective "Phew!" from around the room and they were able to draw a breath again.

"So, let me see if I've got this right," said Clive a little too deliberately. "If it's one of the twins, the camera won't register what we think we see. And if it's neither of the twins, the camera will pick up what we just saw, which is someone looking nondescript."

"That just about sums it up," said Sam.

"And if he was naked?" asked Clive.

"You'd probably think he wasn't there," said Sam.

"Really?" asked Clive disbelievingly.

"I've seen it myself," said Sam. "Pete and I were in the pet shop and Roderick walked up to us and we didn't notice a thing. He showed us the video from a security camera afterwards and he was actually just a few feet away and stark naked."

Sally had been listening with interest. "I like Sam's idea of using the virtual mannequin. We'd obviously need video of the nondescript Roderick – sorry, Roderick – for the therapist and then project that onto the mannequin cut-outs. Then, for the final scene, we could have the twins switching back and forth on the spot – possibly naked if that's okay with everyone – and then seeming to vanish from the stage. It would be hard to pull off, but it'd be sensational if it worked. Lighting would be crucial, though," she added, turning to Geoff. He pulled a tired face, as if already anticipating the extra work he'd have to put into the production.

"Thanks everyone," said Sam. "That's extremely helpful. I suggest we start the read-through. If anyone has any comments or ideas, please pipe up. Jemma has offered to take notes. So, Roderick, over to you. You're in your office and waiting for your new client…"

Two hours later, the read-through was complete and Roderick was walking back to the pet shop. Although Sam's advice had been for him to simply speak the parts, he found himself automatically adding nuances and accents here and there to flesh out the characters. Sam had decided to use 'Rod' and 'Rick' as the names for the twins, and the more Roderick got into character the more these names made sense. But he had a niggling feeling that giving the twins full reign over their identities might prove problematic. As it was, he'd been aware of some resistance from Rick when he left the room as the dark-haired Rod.

As soon as he entered the pet shop, he was greeted by a "Shut that door!" squawk from JG. The parrot had become so much part of the shop's character in just a few days that it would be strange when he had to leave. He'd also had an energising effect on Brian's punctuality and general attitude to his work. If it was possible for a parrot and a human being to become soul mates, they were pretty much there already. He saw that Brian was taking a phone call at the desk and he seemed to be finding the conversation hard going. Brian motioned him over and put his hand over the receiver. "It's some poof talking about a delicious fragrance or something." He handed the phone over to Roderick.

Roderick rolled his eyes upwards in despair at Brian's customer care. "Hello, Roderick Jones here. I'm the owner of the pet shop. How can I help you?"

"Oh, Roderick dear boy. I've heard such fabulous things about you. It's Julian. Julian Simmonds. You won't know me from Adam, of course, but you're looking after our parrot. The thing is that silly queen of a husband of mine has had a heart attack while *in flagrante delicto* with some common trollop of a busboy. I'm beside myself with despair, of course, but it means I'm here with old slack Alice in a fleapit of a hospital and she won't be travelling any time soon."

Somehow Roderick managed to digest all this in a split-second. "I'm so sorry to hear that, Mr Simmonds. It must have been such a shock for you."

"Shock? Oh no, dear boy. Slack Alice is game for anything that's male and moves. If I've seen it once, I've seen it a thousand times. 'Pop-it-in-Pinky', that's what they used to call her when she was delivering her lines for commercials."

Roderick tried to take in the gender role confusion. "Well I do hope your, er, husband recovers soon. And please don't worry about your parrot, we're enjoying having him in the pet shop."

The parrot butted in, "Having him, let's be having him."

"And that lovely boy Pete tells me you're an actor yourself," continued the caller. "It's many years since I trod the boards, of course, but I did make a lovely Iago, if I say so myself. And you're in one of Sam's little plays? Simply splendid. But perhaps a little too modern for us, don't you think?"

By the time the conversation ended, JG's immediate future seemed secure and there was even a suggestion that the parrot should remain in the pet shop if his husband's health remained perilous. Theatrical etiquette also required Roderick to offer them complementary tickets to the production although he doubted they'd bother to attend such a 'little play'.

A try-out in the studio theatre of the same excerpt from *Rosencrantz and Guildenstern Are Dead* demonstrated that Roderick was sufficiently able to cast his spell to the back row of the auditorium. But the closed-minded Clive continued to be the doubting Thomas about Roderick's ability to project himself. So Jemma came up with the cunning plan of offering the audience a free drink before the show to enhance their susceptibility – but one drink only, mind you.

The build-up to the first night was inexorable and more than a little daunting for someone as out of touch with theatrical production as Roderick. Committing just over an hour of script to memory meant many hours spent delivering the words to the occupants of the out-of-hours pet shop, with JG as the chief heckler and critic. But some of the pressure was lifted once the video had been shot of him playing the part of the therapist. And even the sceptical Clive had to admit having Roderick as the virtual therapist with the live Rod or Rick as patient was extremely effective.

Roderick didn't sleep much the night before the play opened. The dress rehearsal had proceeded without any major mishaps. Afterwards, he'd stood in the bitter cold outside the theatre looking at the play's poster and trying to imagine the audience's reaction to seeing one person play three parts. The poster was certainly effective, with the disembodied therapist in the middle, a laptop-illuminated face on the left and an eerie image of a twilight tryst on Hampstead Heath on the right. The play's title 'Tx' certainly gave very little away, which made the whole thing even more tantalising to the viewer. But he couldn't avoid a shiver up his spine seeing his name lit up in bold. A tap on his shoulder alerted him to someone standing next to him.

"You'll do brilliantly, darling," said Sally, the production designer.

He momentarily flipped to Rick and was then back again as Rod.

Sally looked surprised. "Ah, I see what Sam means," she said cryptically.

"What was that?" asked Roderick.

"He said relationships were difficult for you," Sally replied.

"Bloody impossible, actually," said Roderick, turning to look at her. "You know, Sally, I sometimes feel like a fucking freak." He looked back at the poster. "And this could be the biggest mistake of my life. What the hell am I doing, Sally?"

"You're going to prove to the world you're a talented actor who also happens to have something very special up his sleeve," she said reassuringly.

"Yeah, right!" He formed his hand into the shape of a megaphone. "Roll up! Roll up! Come and see the freak show!"

"Well, I don't think you're a freak. Far from it, in fact. And I think you need a drink for your first night nerves."

Sally put a hand on Roderick's shoulder and he accepted the suggestion. They made their way to a nearby pub. "What can I get you?" she asked.

"Well, Rod would simply adore a G&T but Rick insists on a pint of lager," replied Roderick, visibly irritated.

"Okay...," said Sally patiently. "One or the other. Which is it to be?"

Rod became Rick. "Lager please, but you'd better make it a half," he said.

Roderick sat down in a corner of the pub and looked around at the other customers. He recognised a few from the theatre school, including a couple involved in the production, but they hadn't seen him. He glanced at himself in a nearby mirror and noticed he'd reverted into the in-between version. Sally returned with the drinks.

"I almost didn't see you there," she said.

"Yeah, sorry," said Roderick. "The twins are getting burnt out and wanted to lie low for a bit."

Sally looked concerned. "Do you think you'll cope for the entire run?"

"Well, we're all consummate professionals," Roderick replied, taking a sip of the beer. "But don't be surprised if you see me trying to kick my own backside."

"You know, Roderick, something has changed about you," Sally said softly.

"The wiseass, you mean?"

"Something like that. Before, you seemed comfortable with your ability. Now, I'm not so sure. It's almost as if you're fighting it."

"Sorry, I guess that's the story of my life."

"Is that what happened with the production of *Rosencrantz and Guildenstern*?"

"If you mean open rebellion by the twins, then I guess so."

"What will you do once the production is over?"

"I don't know. I suppose I'll return to the pet shop, but it doesn't seem the sanctuary it once was. It's become a little shop of horrors really – another freak show, in fact – and perhaps it needs to go back to selling puppies, kittens and goldfish. It's as if I don't want to surround myself with animals that are as weird as me any longer."

"Couldn't you develop your ability?"

"Possibly, but what would I do with it? The entire cast of *Hamlet* in one? I don't think so."

Sally put a comforting hand on his arm. "Perhaps you need someone to like you just as you are?"

"Is that an offer?"

Sally blushed and removed her hand. "Sorry, I'm crap with relationships myself."

"I think we could both do with seeing a therapist once this is over."

She smiled. "Another half?"

"Okay, but this is Rick's turn and he's having a double G&T."

****

Rod sat on stage waiting to be called into the office by the therapist. He could hear the excited chatter of the audience as they settled into their seats. It was unorthodox to have an actor on stage before the play had even commenced, but there was little that was commonplace about the production. He was flicking through the pages of the latest edition of *Attitude* that the production team had placed in the waiting area of the set. A flat screen TV showed the audience his reading material and the script directed him to linger over pages displaying scantily clad hunks. Titters from the front row indicated approval. He heard a distant bell signalling the five-minute call. The wait seemed interminable and he wished the magazine had more pages. He noticed Sam in the wings giving him a thumbs up sign. The lights in the auditorium finally went down, leaving him in a spotlight. The door to the therapist's consulting room opened. "Please come in, Mr Jones, and make yourself comfortable," announced the disembodied therapist.

Despite the complexities of the production, it all pretty much went like clockwork. As the sole actor, Roderick only had himself to rely on for the timings of entrances and exits. The videoed delivery of the therapist was immutable, of course, but it also served as a reference point. In fact, the virtual mannequin projection was so effective that, at times, Roderick found himself responding to the image as if it were real. Despite Sally's concerns about overtaxing himself, his morphing between the characters seemed effortless.

The technically most demanding scene was that portrayed on the poster: one twin viewing internet porn on the left, the therapist in dialogue with himself and his fantasies, and the other twin pursuing men on Hampstead Heath on the right. Achieving the simultaneous tableaux involved careful separation with lighting, yet more video projection and Roderick dashing across the stage to convince the audience he could be in two places at the same time. The brutal killing of the therapist was staged in a stylised way right out of *Psycho*, with the twins' synchronised stabs coming from either side of the virtual mannequin that ended up drowned in a blood-red wash.

From Roderick's point of view, the trickiest scene for him to pull off was the final one. There'd been discussion about using blow-up dolls to make it appear that there were two people occupying the same area of the stage. In the end, Sam had decided to build on the illusion Roderick used in *Rosencrantz and Guildenstern Are Dead*, keeping his body essentially still and switching between the twins. The fact that he was naked both added to and hindered the illusion. Strobe lighting was the final, dramatic element. For the last few seconds of the play, the twins simply morphed back and forth as fast as possible until the audience was incapable of telling them apart.

The applause was deafening in the small auditorium. Sam joined him on stage and gave him a well-deserved hug. He couldn't help noticing an older, male couple in the front row who had been making good use of a pair of opera glasses and were now giving him a standing ovation.

By the end of the week, Roderick was exhausted. He'd gone through the motions at the end of production party and was uncomfortably aware of the twins jostling for attention. Both his parents and Brian had attended the final performance and he'd convinced himself that outing himself for what he really was could only be for the good. But when his parents came back to his dressing room after the performance it was clear that they'd only seen what they wanted to see. They'd been impressed by the final scene and his mother had even said, "It really looked as if there were two of you, dear." It had never crossed their minds they weren't witnessing anything other than a sophisticated illusion.

The critics had been just as easily hoodwinked. Their praise for the production had been fulsome but they'd been taken in by technical wizardry, and Roderick's own performance had become almost incidental.

The one member of the audience who hadn't been seduced by the smoke and mirrors was Brian, and he knew that from the expression on his face when he took his final bow; the look of open-mouthed awe was just like that of a goldfish.

****

Roderick didn't expect to find the shop door unlocked when he went to work on the Monday. As he entered the shop he felt something had changed. He looked around and noticed that everything seemed more organised and cleaner. He glanced in a few cages and noticed that the animals had already been fed. He smelt freshly-brewed coffee and saw Brian coming towards him with a steaming cup. Brian handed Roderick the cup and smiled. "Respect," he said, placing the fist made from his right hand in the palm of his left hand at stomach level and bowing deeply. "That's Japanese," he added.

"That means a lot to me, Brian," said Roderick, taking a sip of the darkly aromatic contents. He glanced around the shop. "You must have spent hours cleaning and tidying the shop."

"All of yesterday, actually," Brian replied. "I wanted to give you something back after last Friday. You were just amazing."

"And you don't mind I'm a shape-shifter?"

"Respect," Brian replied, bowing again.

Brian returned to the back of the shop where he was cleaning out some cages, leaving Roderick to ponder on what had just transpired. It was clear they'd both seriously underestimated each other.

Drinking his coffee, Roderick turned to the day's mail and noticed a familiar looking envelope with elegant italic writing. There was no stamp, so it had obviously been delivered by hand. He took out the sheet of thick, folded paper and started reading the contents:

Dear Roderick,

I had to drop you a line after your stupendous performance. You probably won't have noticed us, but Markus and I were in the back row for the last night and we were sitting on tenterhooks the entire time. The last scene made me realise what I've been missing for so long. I visited Sparky at Christmas. You wouldn't believe how much he's grown! He probably didn't know me from Adam but I could have sworn the lights on the tree were glowing brighter when he looked at me. Or perhaps he was merely telling me off again.

Have a look at the arts section in today's The Independent.

Love,

Michael

Intrigued, Roderick turned to the arts section of the newspaper. He almost choked on the liquid when he saw what was included in the review section.

Book Review

LIFTING THE LID: The keyboard works of JS Bach uncovered by Michael Brown. A remarkable book that sweeps away the cobwebs of previous scholarship and digs long and deep into Bach's genius. Highly recommended for all lovers of JS Bach.

With that glowing recommendation, Roderick couldn't resist popping along to Blackwell's Bookshop to see whether they had the book in stock. "I'm just going out for a minute," he called out to Brian who gave a thumbs up in reply.

In fact, the bookshop had a stack of them in the window with the sign: 'Local author – Book signing today' prominently displayed. Once inside the bookshop, he noticed an even larger pile of them on a table next to a photograph of the author looking singularly winsome. Hands shaking, Roderick picked up the book and turned the first few pages. His heart beating fast, he read the dedication: 'For Roderick: be true to yourself.'

The shop assistant came over to him, "Are you okay, sir? You look as if you've seen a ghost."

Roderick turned to look at the assistant. "A ghost? Not really. It's just someone I know. He's dedicated the book to me." Roderick pointed at the dedication.

The assistant looked astonished. "You're the actor from the pet shop?"

"Yes, that's me," replied Roderick, and he finally cast aside his guard and walked out of the shop in all his shimmering, shape-shifting, chimeric majesty. The shop assistant had muttered something about a book signing but it didn't register. It was time for Roderick to cash in the rain check. Brian would do a fine job of tending to the shop for the time being.

Chapter 7

Ebenezer

Ebenezer, or, to be precise, Ebenezer *III*, found himself inexorably drawn back to North London. This wasn't through design but more a fact of life given the unpredictability of wormhole transport. In fact, as soon as he'd landed back in the Jin Dynasty *ca.* AD 400, he was whisked away and deposited in a large puddle in an Islington backyard. Fortunately, it had been a very wet autumn and he hadn't come to any harm until another wormhole took him back to the Tang Dynasty *ca.* AD 900

In the half-millennia he'd effectively been away, a crisis had hit the *Carassius auratus auratus* population as a result of Chinese mass-production to meet the demand for ornamental ponds full of orange fish that were believed to bring wealth and prosperity to their owners. Although some believed it was a case of goldfish going on strike for better living conditions, the entire goldfish population had stopped reproducing overnight. Many attempts were made to cajole them with fishy aphrodisiacs, but the goldfish simply wouldn't do the deed that was expected of them.

So, in a last-ditch effort to avoid species extinction and the collapse of the underwater web, Ebenezer had been sent on what could be his final mission back to Islington, AD 2013 to seek out someone who might be able to help.

****

Brian had paid a visit to his aunt's house in an attempt to get better acquainted with her African Grey. He'd taken quite a fancy to JG, the other African Grey, who turned out to be much wiser than his camp repartee had originally suggested. In fact, he really *had* known John Gielgud. So, he wondered whether his aunt's parrot was hiding something equally significant beneath his feathers. And he was – a piece of tuna had escaped his feeding bowl.

The first thing Brian's aunt insisted on when he arrived was making a strong pot of tea and then reading the tea leaves. She wasn't sure what to make of the goldfish shape she saw at the bottom of the cup. Then as soon as Brian got off at Holloway Road tube station, he noticed a hoarding with a huge goldfish trying to sell him something. These coincidences could only mean one thing: Ebenezer was on his way back.

Brian had persuaded Roderick to bid for the Plexiglass tank at an auction. As the former but short-lived home of Jeff (a.k.a. Sparky), it seemed only fitting to buy it for the pet shop. Roderick wasn't entirely sure what he'd put in it, but at a tenth of the cost Mikey had paid for it, it was certainly a bargain. Brian, on the other hand, had a very clear idea of what he intended to do with it and he'd filled the tank with water and some aquatic greenery to await further developments. And at about the time Roderick was doing his final shimmering scene in the dress rehearsal for the play, the development actually started.

Apart from the eerie light coming from a few small fish tanks, the shop was dark and the animals were curled up in their cages. Bruno let forth one of his robust farts in his slumber but it failed to stir the silent air. Suddenly, a glow appeared at the bottom of the Plexiglass tank and then just as quickly disappeared. The addition to the tank gulped a sigh of relief. Ebenezer's worst nightmare was finding himself on a slab of ice in a fishmonger between the smoked haddock and some common-or-garden, farmed salmon. The memory of being in a plastic bag on the back seat of a number ninety-one bus still lingered somewhere in his tiny brain. This tank seemed like heaven, or at least a palatial palace worthy of a goldfish that had travelled through many centuries on a vitally important quest.

When Brian came into work the following morning, he carried out his usual check on the tank. He hadn't expected to see Ebenezer pouting at him through the Plexiglass.

"Fuck, it's you!" he exclaimed delightedly.

A couple of minutes later Brian knew the details of the goldfish's plight. Ebenezer gulped another sigh of relief; he'd done his bit and now it was up to his young friend and the whims of wormholes to decide what happened next. Meanwhile, he was going to enjoy a well-earned rest in his five star accommodation. He wondered how to call for room service.

Brian wasted no time finding goldfish to add to the tank. Ebenezer thought there was a chance the wormhole would return in seven days, so Brian's target was a hundred and fifty goldfish per day. The first thing he did was to scour other pet shops for goldfish, but at two pounds a fish he only had enough money in his bank account to pay for a hundred. He had more success going to a nature reserve in Highbury, where he found hundreds of abandoned goldfish, but it took multiple trips to make the transfer. Ebenezer looked pleased with the progress Brian had made but it still wasn't enough. A "Woof!" from Bruno, who was looking at the tank while stuck to the ceiling, gave Brian an idea.

When Roderick arrived at the pet shop on the morning of the play's last night, he was astonished to see ten dogs waiting patiently outside. One of them had something looking like the tail fin of a fish sticking out of the corner of its mouth. Roderick opened up, disarmed the intruder alarm, and the next thing he knew the dogs were heading for a bucket of water. He was astonished to see the dogs disgorge goldfish out of their mouths into the water and all apparently unharmed. The dogs ambled off just as Brian came into the shop. Roderick heard him make a strange noise the dogs clearly understood, as they immediately galloped off in various directions.

"Morning, Brian. What were the dogs doing?" asked Roderick.

"Nothin' really," he replied, looking a bit shady.

"Er, Brian, I don't think they were doing *nothing*. Ten dogs just deposited goldfish into the bucket over there." He pointed to the left of the shop and in doing so noticed the

Plexiglass tank was no longer empty. "And how come the tank is full of goldfish?"

"It's not full. I still need a few hundred more."

"For what, Brian?"

"Sorry, it's a secret. I've been told not to tell anyone."

"By whom, Brian?"

"That's a secret, too."

Roderick sighed. When Brian was being this evasive, there simply wasn't much point in continuing that line of questioning.

Brian picked up the bucket and emptied the contents into the tank. The dogs would be back later with more goldfish to add to the collection. He'd given up on cats as they'd simply swallow the goldfish. Also the Abyssinian wasn't speaking to him as he'd stopped pretending he was supporting their bid for world domination and the extinction of dogs.

"Oh, by the way, Brian, here's a ticket for tonight's performance. It's in the front row, so you'll have a good view."

Brian dropped the emptied bucket and looked open-mouthed at the ticket, as if it was something from a Wonka bar. "Are you sure?"

"Of course, Brian. I want you to see what I can really do," Roderick said ambiguously.

Actually, what Brian was most surprised by was the golden colour of the complementary ticket, which confirmed to him something very important was about to happen.

****

Brian picked up the newspaper Roderick had been reading just before he left the shop. *So that's why Roderick went out in such a hurry.* But then he became distracted by something happening in the goldfish tank. It had started off as a pound coin-sized area of opalescence in the bottom left but now strange multi-coloured rays of light were stretching out into the rest of the tank. The goldfish clearly knew what was happening as they were lining up in a long, snaking queue to go through wormhole security. Brian considered his options: a) remaining in Islington, North London, assistant to a shape-shifter in a pet shop, hating his family and generally feeling misunderstood by the world; and b) taking the biggest chance of his life and joining the queue to go on the ride of his life and praying he'd grow gills on the way. It was no contest. Brian swiftly undressed and climbed into the tank just as the emanation from the wormhole grew to its maximum.

Brian took a deep breath, held his nose and launched himself towards the bottom left of the tank. It was very cold but his teeth didn't chatter for long. There was a brief swooshing sound followed by a glug and then the tank was empty. The pet shop suddenly became rather peaceful.

****

Roderick walked back into the pet shop. His immediate thought was that another spring clean had taken place while he was away, although it had only been for an hour or so. He'd gone to see Michael but he wasn't at home. He then remembered seeing something about a book signing in the bookshop and realised they'd just missed each other.

As far as Roderick could tell, all the animals were still where they should be but they were strangely silent. He wondered whether Brian had uttered his equivalent of a Hogwarts quietening charm. But, come to think of it, where *was* Brian?

"Brian, I'm back," he called out.

The silence remained unbroken and the animals continued to look dumbstruck. Bruno padded over to him but didn't offer his usual "Woof!" The Tibetan terrier looked up at him with a sorrowful expression and extended a front paw as a greeting. Roderick knelt down to give him a hug.

"Good to see you, old boy. What's happened here?"

Bruno looked dejected and his tail was pointed down. He padded over to the nearest wall and slowly climbed it, then walked across the ceiling until he was suspended above the wet part of the shop. He gave Roderick a strange upside-down look which he took to mean the dog wanted him to see something. Roderick walked over to the row of fish tanks and stopped dead in his tracks. Where there'd been almost a thousand goldfish and hundreds of gallons of water was now just a very large and entirely empty Plexiglass tank. It really *was* as if someone had pulled the plug and the contents had drained away. And he couldn't see any sign of Brian either. It was then he noticed a pile of clothes on the shelf under the tank. Perhaps he should have paid more attention to Brian when he was going on about weird space-time phenomenon. Roderick reached for his mobile phone to call 999.

"Hello, it's Roderick Jones from the pet shop Wet & Wild on Holloway Road. I need to report a missing person. Oh, and about a thousand goldfish have disappeared as well."

That was the easy bit. He didn't know what he'd say to Brian's parents but he'd probably leave out the bit about the goldfish. He wished he'd never done that favour for his aunt.

The ping of the doorbell announced a visitor. Roderick pulled his personas together and put Rick in charge. Dealing with 'London's finest' wasn't straightforward if you mentioned people and goldfish missing in the same breath. The next thing he knew he had someone holding him in a hug and kissing him on the mouth. It wasn't a pretty policeman but it *was* a handsome man in his twenties wearing a dark suit and an open-necked, white shirt. And there wasn't a trace of gel in his hair.

"Gosh, that's a tad more than bromance, Michael," Roderick said, shimmering away.

Michael took a step back and examined Roderick's face. "That's what I love about you, Roderick: three guys for the price of one. I gather I just missed you at the bookshop. A shop assistant there mentioned you'd looked at the book. I think he fancied you."

"I can't believe you dedicated the book to me! In fact, I couldn't believe you wrote the book full stop. I was so surprised I almost stripped off and walked out naked."

Michael's eyebrows rose dramatically. "That would have made his day."

Roderick blushed. "Actually, I went from the bookshop to find you at home."

"Really? You should have phoned first."

"I wanted to surprise you – and to cash in the rain check."

"God, you're adorable." Michael kissed him again. "Anyway, I've come to take you out to lunch. My publisher is paying and there's someone who's keen to meet you. He was in the front row on the last night and enjoyed his eyeful."

"As long as he's not a producer of pornographic paraphernalia."

Michael laughed. "In fact, he *is* a producer but more of the mainstream variety. He's got an idea about teaming up two pianos, a playwright and a shape-shifter."

"Really? With Markus as well?" Michael nodded. "Okay, I'm intrigued. But definitely no animals. And I do have a slight problem to sort out first."

Roderick walked over to the Plexiglass tank where Bruno was still keeping watch.

"Christ, I didn't expect to see the tank again!" exclaimed Michael, looking a bit shaken. "Where did you find it?"

"It was in an auction. Brian persuaded me to buy it for the shop. I wasn't sure why at the time but I think I'm starting to understand now. And it's Brian who's half of the current problem."

"So, what's happened?"

"Brian was up to something while the play was running and filled the tank with hundreds of goldfish. But when I came in just now, the goldfish had vanished along with the water. And the only sign of Brian is that pile of clothes." He pointed at a grey hoodie, some torn jeans and a pair of grubby trainers. There was also a Mickey Mouse watch on top but the second hand was stuck over the bobble on his nose.

Michael scratched his head thoughtfully. "Was he into magic? You know, like Siegfried and Roy and their vanishing elephant."

"Hmm, he had some strange interests but I don't think being an illusionist was quite up his street."

Michael bent down to cautiously inspect the discarded garments. "It's like that film where people just vanish, leaving their clothes behind." He wrinkled his noise at the smell. "Well, his clothes need a wash, that's for sure. Perhaps he simply wanted a bath."

"I suppose bathing with goldfish is the sort of thing Brian *might* do, but if he did get into the tank and he's not pulling a stunt, he must have gone somewhere."

"A rift in space and time, perhaps?" Michael suggested with a grin.

"Well, actually he *was* obsessed with wormholes but it all seemed a bit bonkers to me. In fact, Brian's psychiatrist thought he needed medication."

"Did he ever mention someone called Ebenezer?"

Roderick looked taken aback. "What? How did you know about him?"

"Oh, before I left the house I found an email in my inbox addressed to you. I've printed it out." Michael extracted a piece of folded paper from his jacket pocket and gave it to Roderick to read:

Roderick, So long
And thanks for all the goldfish.
Ebenezer III

"Who was this Ebenezer character, then?" asked Michael.

"A goldfish," replied Roderick, "although I never had the honour of meeting him. Brian talked about him as if he was something special and said he was found on a number ninety-one bus."

Michael shook his head. "That's seriously weird. So what do you think the email means?"

Roderick hesitated before stating the obvious. "Well, it's saying goodbye and thanking me for the goldfish. But it's *from* the goldfish, which is, er, a bit fishy." Michael groaned. "Actually, one of the even fishier ideas Brian had was of the existence of an underwater worldwide web and he believed the goldfish was part of it."

"Christ! It must have been difficult keeping a straight face when he was in full flow."

"It was, but that's where shape-shifting to zone out of the conversation came in handy."

"So, why didn't he send the email direct to you?"

"Well, he was always calling you my boyfriend, so perhaps he was trying to bring us together."

Michael wasn't convinced. "Hmm, I'm sure that's very touching but Brian doesn't comes across as your typical matchmaker. Are you sure he didn't email you as well?"

"I didn't see anything earlier, but I'll check." Roderick went over to his laptop. "No, there's nothing in the inbox, but I'll check the junk... Well, there are some here which look garbled, but there's another that might be similar..." He opened the email. "Yes, it's the same one... Hmm, that's interesting..." He turned to Michael. "Have a look at this, Michael. The syllables in the lines are 5/7/5, which is what you'd find in haiku poems. So, if Brian sent the email, he must be somewhere with internet access. I wonder what the sender's email address was..." They looked at the screen. "That's weird," said Roderick, pointing at the top of the email. "Those characters look like Chinese. How can Brian be sending an email from China?"

"Hold on!" said Michael excitedly. "Look at the time and date. The email was sent last night!"

"Jesus!" exclaimed Roderick. "This is getting crazier by the minute!"

The doorbell pinged again and this time it *was* two police officers waiting at the door. They weren't pretty, their uniforms bulged unflatteringly and they gave the impression of having drawn the short straw.

"Are you Mr Jones?" asked the plumper one of them.

Roderick nodded and shook hands.

"I'm PC Evans and this is" – he turned to his colleague – "PC Samuels. We gather you're reporting a missing person."

"That's right – and also a thousand goldfish."

"A thousand goldfish?" PC Samuels asked incredulously.

"Give or take a few hundred," added Roderick helpfully.

"And where was this person and the goldfish before they disappeared?" asked PC Evans.

"Here." Roderick pointed out the tank and the pile of clothes. The police officers peered inside the tank and then put on latex gloves to inspect Brian's clothes which were still badly in need of a wash.

"How could the goldfish disappear just like that?" asked PC Samuels.

Roderick shrugged. "I don't know, but the person who's gone missing had some pretty far-out ideas about goldfish travelling through time. He also had a strange way of getting dogs to do things for him."

"Would that be Brian Elliott?" asked PC Evans with a look confirming that he'd definitely drawn the short straw.

"Yes. How do you know him?" asked Roderick.

"Oh, the whole family is known to us and particularly his younger brother, Jason," replied PC Evans. He turned to his colleague. "Do you think he's trying to flog goldfish now?"

"No way," replied PC Samuels. "He'd be more likely to eat them than sell them."

"Christ! I've just had a thought!" exclaimed Roderick. "There's a security camera at the back of the shop so maybe it'll show what happened when Brian and the goldfish disappeared."

Roderick led Michael and the police officers to the laptop next to the till. He found the relevant video footage and started the playback. The camera's view faced straight to the front of the shop and the area of interest was on the right. Given the size of the Plexiglass tank and the number of goldfish in it, it wasn't difficult to discern that there had been a full tank of goldfish in the pet shop earlier in the day. Roderick fast-forwarded to the point when he left the shop to go to Blackwell's. The video showed someone wearing a hoodie doing something at the front of the shop and then turning to look at the row of tanks. They caught a brief glimpse of a face.

"Is that Brian Elliott?" asked PC Evans.

"Yes, that's him," Roderick confirmed.

They continued watching. Something was glowing in the largest tank. It was indistinct and the light spreading towards the camera made the video overexposed. But they had no difficulty spotting Brian swiftly take off his clothes and then climb into the tank. The video flared and then abruptly darkened as the camera compensated for a sudden change in light level. The video continued playing just as it was when it started but there was no sign of Brian or the goldfish. The four of them looked at each other.

"Well, I'd say that's indisputable," said PC Evans looking at his colleague.

"But–," said an uncertain PC Samuels who was wondering what he'd write on his report sheet.

"I think we'll leave the rest to the CID," said PC Evans with an air of finality. He turned to Roderick. "And if you don't mind, Mr Jones, please leave everything just as it is. Someone will be around later to take a statement from you and we'll need a copy of the video."

"That's no problem, officer, although we're" – he noticed Michael looking towards the front of the shop – "about to go for lunch. I'll give you my mobile number so you can call me first."

"Er, Roderick you might want to take a look outside," said Michael.

They turned towards the door and saw that the lower part of the windows was obscured by scores of dogs with their muzzles pressed against the glass.

"What the hell?" PC Samuels asked.

They made their way outside. It was hard to say how many dogs were in front of the shop but there were certainly a lot of them and they were obstructing the pavement and therefore constituted a public nuisance. They were still staring into the pet shop. Roderick noticed PC Evans reaching for his radio to report what was happening. He vaguely recalled Brian saying something about being the 'top dog', but he'd dismissed it as just another bizarre idea. Weird as it sounded, perhaps that's why the dogs seemed to be lost and looking for something. An idea occurred to him. He went back into the shop and found

Bruno halfway up a wall trying to get a better look at the commotion outside. He detached him and carried him outside and set him down on the ground. He seemed nervous in the presence of so many dogs and clearly wanted to return to the safety of the shop. Roderick crouched down in front of him and looked in his eyes.

"Christ, Bruno, I wish I knew how Brian did it… Anyhow, here goes…"

Without realising it, Roderick had started shimmering. The two police officers rubbed their eyes and were about to blame the visual aberration on too much overtime. Michael just smiled. Roderick lifted Bruno into place above the mass of dogs and he obediently started to climb the shop window. The dogs stopped looking into the shop and craned their necks to follow his progress.

"Good boy, Bruno!" Roderick called encouragingly.

Bruno turned slowly and carefully until he was facing the mob. He extended his head and looked left and right, as if surveying his troops. "Woof! Woof!" he went. Within seconds, as if a spell had been broken, the dogs dissipated and went their separate ways. Bruno descended to applause from onlookers on both sides of the road who'd been recording the action on their phones. *Oh shit, that's definitely broken the Official Secrets Act*, thought Roderick.

PC Samuels and PC Evans decided they needed a beer, even if they were technically still on duty. In the space of an hour, they'd seen a naked man and a thousand goldfish vanish before their eyes, a pack of dogs window shopping, a pet shop owner shimmer and then a dog climb a shop window and dispel a mob of dogs with a bark.

"Come on, Bruno, we're going for some lunch," said Michael as Roderick shut up the shop. "Perhaps the production could be two pianos, a playwright, a shape-shifter and an aerobatic dog?"

"Definitely no animals! I'm sticking to humans for the time being," replied Roderick, kissing his boyfriend for the very first time in public. There was a brief shimmer of resistance from Rick but Rod wasn't going to let him ruin the occasion.

Roderick and Michael walked off down Holloway Road, hand-in-hand, back to the bookshop with Bruno trotting happily along beside them, pleased to be elevated to the position of top dog and looking forward to some leftovers from his master's table. And he thought his master's new friend was rather nice, too.

****

Back in the shop, dust motes lazily stirred in the sunlight streaming through the windows. The animals in their cages and tanks were enjoying a brief respite from all the recent comings and goings. The infrared detectors of the intruder alarm remained ever vigilant, scanning for any unusual activity. Over in the far left corner, something *was* stirring but the detectors didn't register anything. The dust motes were motionless above the Plexiglass tank as if standing guard ready for someone important to appear. All of a sudden, the tank was no longer empty.

Brian felt down the length of his body, disappointed he still hadn't grown gills but relieved he hadn't drowned. Riding a wormhole was definitely loads better than Nemesis at Alton Towers. And it hadn't involved an argument with his dad to get him to pay for it. He eased himself carefully out of the tank, looking around the shop. Immediately the detectors registered the new presence and the alarm bell started ringing stridently. Still naked, Brian ran to the front of the shop and entered the code to cancel the alarm. Silence was restored to the shop. He checked the front door and found it was locked. *Roderick must have gone out for lunch*, he decided. That reminded him how hungry he was. He walked back to the tank and found the pile of his clothes where he'd left them. Someone had rummaged through them as it wasn't the neat pile he'd left. He sniffed his hoodie: still the same smell and it needed a wash. His watch was showing the wrong time.

His clothes back on, Brian went to the kitchenette at the rear of the shop and inspected the contents of the fridge. He found a half-full can of tuna left behind from when he was still friends with cats. He dug into the tuna with his fingers, devouring the fish hungrily. He felt as if he hadn't eaten for days. He stood up and looked at himself in the mirror above the sink: he definitely needed a shave and somehow he looked a bit older and wiser.

Brian realised he hadn't said hello to the animals in the shop since he'd returned, so he went over to the golden retriever he'd rescued from the council house. The dog looked up at him wistfully and gave him a whining yelp, as if needing to understand why his former human owner could treat him so badly. Brian knelt down and opened the cage door to take him into his arms. Dog and human nuzzled each other. Brian held the dog's head gently in his hands and looked into its deep, dark eyes. He saw the despair the dog felt during its weeks of incarceration. Tears trickled down his cheeks. "I won't let that sort of thing ever happen to you again. I promise that," he said softly. Both dog and human looked puzzled. *That's weird,* he thought. *I'm thinking in English, so why am I speaking something that sounds like Chinese?* Dog and human looked at each other again and agreed that sometimes words just got in the way.

Author's Note

Chapter One

A real-life Doctor Dolittle would have their work cut out for them, as the animal kingdom uses widely varying means of communication from species to species. Although there have been numerous claims to communicate with animals by psychic means, any proof remains entirely circumstantial and is bound to be a matter of wishful thinking and suggestibility. Communication at a more emotional level, including that involving humans with autistic spectrum disorders, may be more fruitful, but would be limited to those animals that can actually emote.

The debate about the relative intelligence of cats and dogs has endured for centuries. Although a dog's brain (e.g. a beagle) is double that of a domestic cat (seventy-two grams vs. thirty grams), a cat's cerebral cortex has double the number of neurons of a dog's brain, which would suggest a greater capacity for information processing. Some researchers have suggested dogs have become dumbed-down because of too much domestication and dependency on humans. In contrast, cats have been allowed to do their own thing for far too long and have never been encouraged to develop intellectual powers. However, even if cats were trained up, it seems far-fetched to believe the 'assistance cat', 'police cat' or 'search and rescue cat' will ever take off – or that cats would deign to allow it.

And would cats and dogs ever work together? Well, cats have certainly been known to climb onto a dog's back to catch a lift, so climbing up an Irish wolfhound's back isn't that far-fetched. There's also a video on YouTube of a cat climbing its scratch pole to twist open the doorknob to let its doggie pal out of the kitchen.

Chapter Two

Electricity was viewed as almost mystical in the eighteenth century, so an animal capable of generating electricity was manna from heaven for quacks and purveyors of amusement. Electric eels were introduced to London society in the 1770s and their popularity was such that 'electric eel parties' became all the rage, with many guests vying to join hands together to receive 'therapeutic' shocks. Although more than two centuries have passed, the electric eel still occupies a unique position in the animal kingdom, with several reclassifications to place it in the most appropriate taxonomic group.

Harnessing the discharges produced by an electric eel to generate electricity sounds fanciful, but a YouTube video shows an electric eel in an aquarium in Tokyo lighting up a Christmas tree in December 2007. A few years before his death in 2004, eccentric Hollywood legend Marlon Brando summoned the actor Ed Begley Jr to his Mulholland Drive home to discuss his scheme of powering his home with electric eels. In reality, hundreds of electric eels would be required. Also, the food bill would exceed the cost of the electricity in the first place. But, like photovoltaic cells, electric eels could trickle charge a battery to supplement an existing mains power supply. Other possibilities include a biomimetic power source that's modelled on the electric eel's electrocytes and even mapping the eel's genome to engineer a 'bio-battery'.

The final word on the subject goes to the British architect Catrina Stewart, who proposes a self-sufficient electric eel lift: "A conventional elevator in a 20-floor apartment block will use 100 watt hour per round trip. 20 eels, producing 500-watt hour each time they move, should ensure that the lift is constantly moving. When the lift stalls, the eels will need to be woken up and excited to get the lift moving again." Brilliant.

Chapter Three

Aside from being revered and then mummified by Egyptian society, cats have had a raw deal down the ages. In fact, up until 1817, they were thrown from a tower in Ypres, Belgium in the belief that witchcraft was expunged by their death.

Although cats are typically aloof when exposed to human emotions, there have been unusual cases where a cat has given the impression of something extrasensory occurring. This was explored in a book entitled *Do Cats Have ESP?* that detailed stories of felines with supposedly mystical powers. Unfortunately, the author – a 'legendary' American psychic – read too much into her tea leaves and the book lacked a jot of credibility. The simple answer is, of course, "No, they don't." But I was still intrigued by the idea of 'what if?' And putting a cat (but not that belonging to Schrödinger) in a Faraday cage appealed.

What cats *do* have are enhanced senses, including the widest hearing range of nearly any mammal, exceptional eyesight and an extra olfactory organ and an unusual interest in sex? Well, even the most randy tomcat would view human sexual activity in the same disdainful way as any other human behaviour that doesn't immediately impact on him. There have been reports of cats appearing unusually interested in human mating behaviour, but that probably comes down to the particular pheromones being released by an amorous couple.

It is also worth remembering that cats are fundamentally carnivorous and their survival instinct will cause them to turn to whatever is available if their usual supply of food dries up. Dogs will usually wait for several days before feeding off a recently-deceased owner; cats simply do what comes naturally to them.

Chapter Four

The average seventy-gram gecko's footpads are thought to be capable of supporting a weight of a hundred and thirty-three kilograms. Each of the millions of setae on each toe of the gecko forms a self-cleaning dry adhesive on virtually any surface. This can include a vertical sheet of glass or the side of a building. The development of synthetic setae is well underway and diverse applications envisaged include fumble-free football gloves, rock-climbing aids and robot window cleaners. Stanford University's 'Stickybot' is a robot that's remarkably similar to a gecko both in appearance and function. Their 'Stickybot III' is climbing ever higher up even more challenging surfaces and enjoying frequent outings on YouTube. Not surprisingly, the 'Stickybot' research is funded by the US Department of Defense who probably envisage sending in armed gecko robots to scale despot's palaces. The Department of Defense would doubtless also be interested in a transgenic dog if it were equipped with gecko footpads. If nothing else, the traction of a pack of Siberian huskies on icy surfaces would be improved. Thus far, a cloned beagle called Ruppy, 'born' in the labs of South Korea, has been transgenically equipped with a fluorescent gene which means its body glows oh-so-usefully under ultraviolet light. In theory, the genes coding for a gecko's setae could be added to a cloned dog's DNA in the same way as fluorescence genes. But it's anyone's guess as to what phenotype might emerge out of the merger of reptilian and mammalian genes.

Chapter Five

It's commonly assumed all chameleons share the ability to alter their appearance according to their immediate surroundings. In fact, of 160 species of chameleons, few can achieve the full variation in colouration and pattern attributed to this member of the iguana family. The main purpose of the camouflage is to avoid predators, although it also has functions in social signalling and in response to temperature. A species like Smith's dwarf chameleon is able to fine-tune their camouflage according to the vision of the particular predator involved.

The mechanism of the colour change involves three layers of specialised chromatophore cells below the chameleon's transparent outer skin. The colour changes occur in response to nerve signals from the chameleon's brain and the response time can be in the millisecond range.

The idea of harnessing the chameleon's technique to create a sort of cloaking device is an attractive one. However, the physiology and biochemistry of colour changing is complicated. Multiple genes are probably involved and splicing the genes into another organism is likely to be a fruitless enterprise. After all, a prerequisite is transparent skin and there's little of that in the animal kingdom.

On the other hand, using technology to do something similar is a much more practical proposition. In 2011, BAE Systems introduced *Adaptiv* infrared camouflage technology which uses thousands of hexagonal panels to cover the sides of a tank, helicopter or boat. The panels are rapidly heated and cooled to match either the temperature of the vehicle's surroundings or one of the objects in the thermal cloaking system's database, such as a truck, car, large rock or even a cow. Other researchers in New Mexico are developing synthetic, biomimetic materials which adaptively colour shift and can become fabrics worn in combat.

Chapter Six

The internet is replete with paranoid conspiracy theories about 'shape-shifters' or beings with the ability to switch between distinct appearances. And rather more than healthy attention centres on the supposition of reptilian aliens who've successfully made their way into the highest echelons of politics, royalty and commerce. Devising plausible science for shape-shifting seemed a tall order, so I was drawn to consider how people might be manipulated into thinking shape-shifting had occurred. Some sort of mental imprinting onto the viewer's visual cortex seemed to be the most appealing mechanism.

'Human spontaneous invisibility' has been written about for centuries, including in Hinduism, where a combination of concentration and meditation is said to make the body imperceptible to other people. One contemporary account includes someone at a party trying to communicate with other guests and apparently not being seen or heard. On another occasion, a woman stole from a department store as a college prank but the police were oblivious of her presence in the store or the police station. Of course, there's no likelihood corporeal invisibility is achieved, but a combination of how the individual behaves and the susceptibility of the intended audience might explain the phenomena.

I also liked the idea of combining this mental invisibility cloak with a human genetic chimera, the two genotypes in the one individual asserting their fully developed phenotypes through the power of concentration with a hint of Cyril-like ESP. Most chimeras go through life without realising they are chimeras, and may have minor differences corresponding to the two sets of chromosomes, such as differential hair growth on opposite sides of the body, or eyes of dissimilar colours. More extreme manifestations include intersex conditions and even true hermaphroditism. Roderick's situation wouldn't come under any intersex condition; in my world, he's bisexual because of his contrasting sets of chromosomes, although that's not a real theory of sexuality I'd want to posit.

Chapter Seven

Goldfish do actually date back to the Jin Dynasty (265–420), although it wasn't until the Tang Dynasty (618–907) that the gold variety became popular through the equivalent of modern-day fish farming.

Goldfish have the capacity to grow to a considerable size if fed the right diet and kept in the right environment. A fish named 'Goldie', kept in a tank in Folkestone, Kent, measured at fifteen inches in length and weighed just over two pounds. But most goldfish don't have a luxurious lifestyle and only grow to a couple of inches.

Although a goldfish's brain is tiny (0.1 gram), they're actually quite bright as fish go and can even learn tricks. Goldfish are generally thought to have a memory span of about three months, which would make them quite useful as transporters of information in an underwater worldwide web, as memories would simply self-destruct ready for the brain to be filled up with new information.

Wormholes undoubtedly do exist somewhere in the universe although they're often inconveniently near a black hole, which means no sooner you've arrived at your destination, you'd be sucked into a black hole and gone for good, which wouldn't be the sort of holiday you'd want to write home to your folks about.